The
Very Best
Hanukkah
Gift

The Very Best Hanukkah Gift

Joanne Rocklin

Illustrated by
Catharine O'Neill

A Yearling Book

35 Years of Exceptional Reading

Yearling Books
Established 1966

Published by
Dell Yearling
an imprint of
Random House Children's Books
a division of Random House, Inc.
1540 Broadway
New York, New York 10036

Visit us on the Web! www.randomhouse.com/kids

Educators and librarians, for a variety of teaching tools, visit us at
www.randomhouse.com/teachers

ISBN 0-440-41554-3

Reprinted by arrangement with Delacorte Press

Printed in the United States of America

September 2001

10 9 8 7 6 5 4 3 2

OPM

For Eric, who also loves stories
—J.R.

Contents

The
Very Best
Hanukkah
Gift

WEDNESDAY
Green and Gross

It was the first night of Hanukkah at last. Daniel Bloom felt as if he had been waiting forever. Candlelighting! Stories! Gifts! He raced into the kitchen to see what was for dinner. He knew it would be extra-special. Sure enough, a big platter of pancakes sat on the counter.

"Potato *latkes*! Whoopee!" said Daniel.

But something was wrong. Very wrong. His older brother, Jonah, and little sister,

Amy, were sitting at the kitchen table with grumpy looks on their faces.

"Don't get too excited," Jonah said. "Those *latkes* are really gross."

Mrs. Bloom bent down to check on the chicken roasting in the oven. "They are not gross. You haven't even tasted them yet."

"I don't have to taste them," said Jonah. "You know why? They're green! Who ever heard of green *latkes*?"

Daniel was shocked. "Green?" he asked. "What do you mean?"

He took a closer look. Jonah was right. The *latkes* had little green flecks in them.

"Mommy got the *latkes* at the zoo. They're zoo-cchini!" said Amy, tossing her red curls and giggling at her own joke.

"Excuse me, zucchini *latkes* are nothing to laugh about," Jonah said. "Zucchini *latkes* are sad. Very sad."

"Mom!" cried Daniel. "It's not really Hanukkah without potato *latkes*!"

"Don't worry. It's really Hanukkah,"

said his mother. "I just thought it would be fun to try something different. I think you'll like these." She covered the platter with foil and put it in the top oven to warm. "Now, all of you, please set the table."

"At least we're having chocolate cupcakes for dessert," grumbled Jonah.

"Green and gross! Gross and green! Weirdest *latkes* I've ever seen!" said Daniel as he put down the silverware at each setting on the dining room table.

Nothing else seemed to be different this Hanukkah, Daniel noticed with relief.

There was the same blue-and-white HAPPY HANUKKAH sign looped across the doorway to the living room. Although this year a torn leg of one *K* dangled forlornly. He would tape it later.

On a table in the living room was the large, freshly polished family menorah. Beside it were Daniel's and Jonah's smaller menorahs, which their parents had bought when they each turned five. All set to light, Daniel noted with satisfaction. Each menorah held one candle on the far right and the *shammes* candle, which was used to light the other candles, in the center space.

And there, in a corner of the dining room, was the big pile of wrapped gifts from his parents, grandparents, and brother and sister. One for each night of Hanukkah for each kid. Three kids. Eight nights. That was—

"There are twenty-two gifts," said Jonah, as if he were reading Daniel's mind. "There should be twenty-four. *Someone*'s gifts aren't out there yet."

"I know *that*," Daniel said. Or he probably *would* have got the math right, if Jonah hadn't interrupted his calculations. Sometimes Jonah thought he knew everything just because he was ten, two whole years older than Daniel.

"And don't worry," said Daniel guiltily. "My gifts for you and Amy will be ready very soon. I'm still working on them."

Daniel eyed the gift pile carefully. One of the packages was probably the Space Explorer CD-ROM he wanted. Probably that flat, square one!

"Green and gross, gross and green!" sang Daniel cheerfully, laying down the napkins.

Mr. Bloom came into the room, carrying another small menorah.

"Whose menorah is that?" asked Daniel.

"It's Amy's. She can light her own this year too," said Mr. Bloom.

"She *can*?" asked Daniel, surprised.

"I'm five now, don't forget!" said Amy, running over. "I'm growing up, up, up!" She carefully placed her menorah on the table beside her older brothers'.

How come Amy seems to be getting older so quickly? Daniel thought. He himself felt stuck at being eight years old forever. He went over to the table and picked up his own menorah. With his fingernail he scraped off an old piece of melted wax left over from last year's candlelighting. Last year seemed long ago, but nothing much had changed. He still wasn't so hot at math, for instance. Jonah still beat him at arm wrestling. But he could crack his knuckles now, Daniel reminded himself. And his feet had grown one whole shoe size.

But last year he wasn't afraid of dogs. This year he was, ever since that mean dog bit him in the park last summer. And now there was the big new dog that had just moved into the apartment next door! Daniel shivered. He would try not to think about dogs. Not tonight.

Amy was growing up, but sometimes Daniel felt as if he were sort of growing *down*.

Jonah ran to the window. "It's dusk," he said. "Can we light the candles now?"

"Yes, it's time to begin," said Mrs. Bloom.

Everyone crowded around as Mr. And Mrs. Bloom helped the children light their *shammes* candles. They all chanted the blessings together, beginning with

"*Barukh atah Adonai
Eloheinu melekh ha-olam*

Asher kidshanu b'mitzvotav
V'tzivanu
L'hadlik ner shel Hanukkah."

Then, with the *shammes* candles, the first night's candles were lit. The flames danced and the menorahs sparkled.

I feel like I'm in an enchanted room, thought Daniel. Everything looked different in the soft candlelight. Wouldn't it be great if they could light the Hanukkah candles every single night of the year? Of course, then the candles wouldn't be special. They would be as ordinary as the rug on the floor, which he hardly ever noticed.

Mr. and Mrs. Bloom sat down on the sofa to begin the storytelling. "Thousands of years ago . . . ," said Mrs. Bloom as Amy snuggled beside her.

Daniel and Jonah lay down comfortably on the rug. Daniel loved listening to all his parents' stories, but the story of Hanukkah was one of his favorites.

". . . mean Atiochus, King of the Syrians, ruled the Jewish people of ancient Israel," continued his mother. "The Jews worshiped their own God. They had their own customs, language, and temples."

"Antiochus didn't like that one bit," said Mr. Bloom. "Nosiree. He wanted everyone in his kingdom to think and act and believe exactly the same way."

"Bo-ring," said Daniel from down on the floor.

"Right," said Mr. Bloom. "But Antiochus thought it would be easier to rule if everyone had the same customs and beliefs. He ordered the Jews to burn their holy books and stop observing their religious laws. And he killed those who didn't obey."

"I would run away!" said Amy with a frown. She moved closer to her father on the sofa. "I would run away and hide and never come out."

Daniel smiled to himself. Amy was only five. She didn't remember that the best part of the story was coming.

"Some of the Jews *did* hide, but they had a plan," said Mrs. Bloom. "One brave man, Mattathias, fled to the mountains and caves with his five sons. They organized an army. When Mattathias died, his son Judah took over as leader. Judah's nickname was Maccabee, which means 'hammer' in Hebrew. That's why all of Judah's men were called Maccabees."

"Okay, here comes the part about the elephants," said Daniel.

"Elephants!" exclaimed Amy. "What elephants?"

"Shhh!" said Jonah.

"Antiochus's army was huge," said Mr. Bloom. "His soldiers had fancy weapons, and yes, they had elephants. Thirty-two of them, which marched into battle too. But Antiochus and his elephants didn't stand a chance against that little band of fearless Maccabees, nosiree!"

Daniel closed his eyes. He imagined the noisy, scary battle scenes. How wonderful to be so fearless!

And finally came the part of the story that sent shivers up and down Daniel's spine.

"Well, when the victorious Maccabees returned to their temple, they found it in ruins," said Mrs. Bloom.

"Smashed, bashed, and totally trashed by their enemies," said Mr. Bloom. "Dirt and ashes were everywhere."

Shiver.

"So they cleaned everything up and built a new altar," said Mrs. Bloom. "They searched and found only one tiny vial of holy oil to light the temple's menorah."

Shiver, shiver.

"It was only enough oil for one day. But—"

"The oil burned for eight days," Daniel couldn't help interrupting his mother. "A miracle!"

"And that's why we celebrate the holiday for eight days," said Mr. Bloom. Then he held up one of the gold-foil–wrapped chocolate coins from the bowl on the coffee table. "The Maccabees threw away all their gold coins with nasty Antiochus's face on them. They put Judah Maccabee's image on their own coins. And that's why we sometimes give money, called *gelt,* at Hanukkah. Or chocolate *gelt,* like these. And of course we exchange other gifts, too."

Daniel glanced at the gift pile. Which gift would he open first? He could hardly wait. His stomach rumbled. He could probably eat that whole bowl of chocolate coins all by himself!

"And to remember the miracle of the oil, we light candles," said his mother. "And we eat fried foods, like *latkes.* Even zucchini *latkes,*" she said with a grin.

Daniel's stomach rumbled again. He could even eat one of those green things, that was how hungry he was!

Jonah shook his head skeptically. "Well, I'm sorry, but I'm older and wiser now. I just don't believe it," he said.

"What do you mean?" asked Daniel, sitting up and staring at his brother.

"Maybe the oil had been lying around in

the sun and it got sort of concentrated or something. Maybe it lasted because of chemistry," said Jonah. "Nobody knew anything about science in those olden times. It wasn't a miracle at all."

Daniel wondered if anyone else had ever had that thought before. True, Jonah had his own chemistry set, a Hanukkah gift from last year. But was Jonah *that* smart? Smarter than Rabbi Feldman? Daniel liked the story much better the old way. He decided that nobody was going to change it.

"Maybe it was a miracle just because it *happened*," he said. "They found the oil just when they needed it. So what if it was chemistry?"

"Science and miracles," said Mr. Bloom, smiling at his sons. "Maybe both at the same time?"

Jonah looked thoughtful. "Maybe," he said.

"Okay, open your presents now. Then let's eat!" said Mrs. Bloom.

Amy got a doll and Jonah a book. Daniel

decided to save the flat, square box for another night, since he sort of knew what it was. He chose to unwrap an intriguingly long, skinny one.

Socks, from his Grandma Fritzie in Florida. *Oh, well,* Daniel thought. There were seven more nights to come.

"See if your new socks fit," said his mother.

Daniel tried them on. "They fit fine," he said.

At dinner Daniel stared at the green-flecked zucchini *latke* beside the chicken leg on his plate. Curious, he took a bite of the *latke,* chewing slowly.

"Not bad!" he said, surprised. "Actually, delicious."

"Not bad at all," said Jonah, his mouth full.

"Another miracle," said their mother.

Soon only one zucchini *latke* was left on the platter.

"It belongs to Daniel," said Jonah, who had been keeping track.

"I'm leaving room for dessert," said Daniel, leaning back contentedly in his chair. "I think I'll have the *latke* as an after-school snack tomorrow." And he wrapped it in his napkin.

After dinner there would be a treasure hunt for chocolate Hanukkah *gelt,* just like every year. Daniel wriggled his feet in his soft new socks. He watched the candles grow smaller and smaller, still flickering merrily.

Zucchini or potato *latkes*—it didn't matter at all. It was really Hanukkah.

THURSDAY
That Dog

Crunch. Crunch.

Daniel's boots made crunching noises on the snow-packed sidewalk.

He knew there would be one thousand and fifty-five crunches if he took the short-cut home. And two thousand and seventy crunches if he took the long way. But no matter which way he took, short or long, no matter how many crunches, he still had to get there.

And face that dog next door. That *huge*

dog next door. Daniel hadn't actually seen it yet, but he could tell by its bark that the dog was enormous.

Crunch. Crunch. Daniel decided to take the long way home, through the park.

"Pretend you're a Maccabee soldier," his older brother, Jonah, had advised him the night before. "I bet that will help build up your courage."

"How do I do that?" Daniel had asked.

"You could recite that poem from *The Happy Hanukkah Holiday Book*."

"Which poem?"

"I can't believe you forgot it," Jonah had said. "We read it every year."

"Well, I did forget it," Daniel had answered. "A year is a long time."

Jonah himself hardly forgot anything. Squaring his shoulders, he had waved and thrust with an imaginary sword.

"I am a Maccabee.
Brave and tall,

I fight for freedom
For us all!"

Then Jonah had jumped onto Daniel's bed and waved his pretend sword under Daniel's nose.

> *"Maccabees, hey!"*

Wave.

> *"Maccabees, ho!"*

Wave.

> *"Maccabees, Maccabees,*
> *Here we go!"*

Wave, wave.

"Okay, okay, I get the idea," Daniel had said.

Daniel had looked at the pictures in *The*

Happy Hanukkah Holiday Book. Then he had read the Maccabee poem a couple of times before turning off the light. To build up his courage, just in case Jonah was right.

Crunch. Crunch.
But he wasn't a Maccabee.

Maccabees were tall, muscled men with beards, Jewish soldiers who had lived long ago. They wore white outfits that looked like skirts and carried swords to fight their enemies. They were brave and strong.

He, on the other hand, was an eight-year-old boy on his way home from school in modern times. Wearing a faded ski jacket that used to belong to his brother. He didn't have a sword. He didn't have big muscles. And he wasn't brave, that was for sure.

Daniel's breath met the cold air in thin white puffs.

"I am a dragon, breathing smoke and fire!" Daniel growled.

He imagined himself with pointy yellow

teeth and giant claws. With his long, scaly tail, Daniel the Dragon would snatch up that huge dog. The dog would squirm and struggle to get free.

"No mercy for you! *Aargh!*" Daniel would roar.

And swallow the dog in one slurpy gulp. *Crunch. Crunch.*

But he wasn't a dragon, either.

Daniel had reached the park. He flopped down into a snowbank. He made a few snow angels, then sat up and looked around sheepishly. Had anyone seen him? He hoped not. Making angels in the snow was babyish. Fun, though. Were things more fun back when he was a baby? Or even when he was a little kid, like his sister, Amy?

Sometimes it seemed like it. But sometimes he still felt like a baby, at least where dogs were concerned.

Daniel sighed. He brushed the snow off his jacket. He had to go home sometime.

Tonight was the second night of Hanukkah. They would light the candles and open gifts, and this time there would be potato *latkes* for dinner.

He had to admit that last night's zucchini *latkes* hadn't been so bad. Daniel took his leftover zucchini *latke* from his backpack. He took a big bite of it. That made him feel much better. He put the rest into his pocket and headed home.

Crunch. Crunch.

Mr. Rumper, the super, was shoveling snow from the front walk of Daniel's apartment building.

"Lots of snow expected this week, David," said Mr. Rumper, who never seemed to remember Daniel's name.

Daniel took his key from his pocket and trudged slowly up the walk. He unlocked the big front door of the apartment building.

Lately he heard the barking and growling even before he got off the elevator at the second floor. Daniel listened. Nothing. Maybe they weren't home! He started down the hallway.

But today the door of the new tenants' apartment was wide open! Daniel's heart began to hammer. The palms of his hands began to sweat. And then he remembered. Dogs can smell fear.

Daniel took a deep breath. *Calm down,* he told himself. *Walk slowly and quietly. Try, try, try not to smell like fear.*

But there, right in front of him, was that dog!

Daniel stopped walking. He felt as if he had stopped breathing, too.

The dog began lumbering toward him, a huge reddish brown blur. *Thump, thump.* Its feet thumped the floor loudly. Soon the dog would be so close Daniel would see the drool at the side of its mouth. Then he would see its fangs and long, pimply tongue and feel its hot, sour breath. And then he would feel the bite. It was happening all over again!

Daniel froze like a statue. He wanted to run, but his arms and legs just weren't working.

The dog barked hoarsely.

"Rusty? Let me put on your leash," a voice called from inside the apartment.

The dog turned toward the voice, then back to Daniel. Its big, dark eyes met Daniel's in a threatening gaze. Daniel's heart pounded. Then, just as the dog started to come closer, Daniel smelled something.

It was something familiar and wonderful, wafting toward him from his own apartment next door. That smell made him remember what Jonah had told him. It made him remember what he had in his pocket.

"*Maccabees, hey!*" yelled Daniel as loudly and fiercely as he could. And he threw his zucchini *latke* right at the dog.

"Grr-ump?" went Rusty, sniffing at the pancake.

Daniel backed away slowly. Then he quickly turned and raced toward the smell of those potato *latkes* and home.

FRIDAY
Daniel's Maccabee

Early the next morning Daniel had a dream.

It was a hot summer day at the park. Daniel-in-the-dream ran to the water fountain. He was so thirsty! To his surprise, a sign said DOGS ONLY. STAY AWAY.

"Some joke!" said Daniel.

He leaned over to take a drink. A dog was lying beneath the fountain. Daniel bent down to pet it. Too late, he remembered he should never pet strange dogs. And this was the strangest dog he'd ever seen! Its fur was zucchini green and it had little orange ears. Its eyes flashed fire.

Suddenly the dog growled, as if to say, "This is *dog* territory!" It lunged at Daniel's ankle. Its yellow fangs glinted in the sunlight.

"Go away!" Daniel yelled when he felt the bite. He shook his leg as hard as he could. The dog raced away.

And then Daniel woke up. His head hurt and his mouth was dry. He got out of bed and dressed slowly for school, thinking about his scary dream.

"You were hollering in your sleep again," Jonah told him at breakfast.

"I was?" Daniel asked. "What did I say?"

"You said, 'Go away!' and then, 'Grumble, mumble, grumble.' I couldn't really understand you."

"Daniel has bad dreams, Veronica," Amy explained in a loud whisper to her new doll.

"Oh, honey, was it that dream about the dog again?" asked his mother.

"Yes," said Daniel. "Everything was just like it happened in real life."

Well, almost. The dog that bit him last summer hadn't been green like a zucchini, with little orange ears.

"Daniel's afraid of dogs, Veronica," whispered Amy to her doll. "A bad dog bit him last summer at the park. After that, he was afraid to go outside. Sometimes he didn't even want to go to school."

"Cut that out!" said Daniel. "You don't have to tell her *everything*!"

"Yes, I do," Amy said. "Veronica's new around here."

"She's only a *doll*, guys!" said Jonah, laughing.

"I don't care," said Daniel, even though he knew Jonah was right.

Daniel's mother and father looked at each other. Daniel understood that look. It was their "worried about Daniel" look. Lately they acted as if Daniel, not Amy, was the youngest child in the family.

"Did I ever tell you what used to scare me when I was a kid?" asked his father.

Ordinarily Daniel loved his father's "did I ever tell you" stories. But this morning Daniel was grumpy. And his head was pounding.

"Probably," he said.

"You never told *me*," said Jonah.

Mr. Bloom carefully buttered a piece of toast. "You may not believe this. Promise not to laugh?"

"*We* promise!" said Amy, waving Veronica.

Daniel shrugged.

Mr. Bloom bit into his toast and chewed. "I used to be afraid of clowns," he said finally.

"*Clowns?*" asked Daniel incredulously.

"A clown bit you?" asked Amy.

Daniel and Jonah laughed. Now Daniel felt like Amy's big brother again.

"No, a clown never bit me," said Mr.

Bloom. "But it was a clown who lit the match just before the Great Alphonso was shot out of the cannon at the circus. I was six years old. What a noise that cannon made! And there was poor Al, flying from one end of the circus tent to the other! I almost fell out of my seat. After that, I could never look at a clown without shaking. And they *are* kind of scary looking, you have to admit."

"So then what happened?" asked Daniel, picking at his cereal. His throat felt scratchy.

Mr. Bloom thought for a moment. "Well, I guess I just grew out of it."

"But how?" Daniel asked.

His father looked stumped and took another bite of his toast. Daniel was surprised. Usually his dad had an answer for everything.

"I'm not sure how I did it, kiddo," Mr. Bloom said gently. "I'll try to remember."

Daniel put his head down on the table. "I'm not feeling very well," he said.

"Really?" asked Mrs. Bloom.

"Really," said Daniel. "I promise I'm not faking."

His mother put a cool hand on his forehead. "Oh," she said. "You do feel warm."

She brought Daniel the thermometer. He kept it in his mouth for three minutes by the kitchen clock.

"Ninety-nine point nine," said Jonah, reading the thermometer over his mother's shoulder. "One point three degrees above normal."

Mrs. Bloom looked worried. "I have that big meeting today," she said. "I really have to go to work."

"No problem," said Mr. Bloom. "Daniel and I will stay home together. I have some phone calls I can make from here."

Jonah looked at Daniel enviously. "You get to try out your new Space Explorer CD-ROM!" he said.

But Daniel didn't really feel like playing with his Hanukkah present. When his mother had left for work, and his brother and sister for school, he lay down on the living room couch.

"I'll be on the phone in the kitchen if you need me," said his father.

"Okay," said Daniel. He closed his eyes. He listened to the gentle murmuring of his father on the telephone. He could hear the honking drone of the traffic outside.

Pretty soon he heard the marching of elephants.

Thump. Thump. Thump.

Elephants? Daniel-in-the-dream sat up. A tired-looking man in a white outfit was drinking at that same water fountain in the park.

"You're a Maccabee!" said Daniel.

The man stopped drinking. "I sure am," he said, looking surprised. He wiped his mouth with the back of his sunburned hand. "But how did you know?"

"Oh, I've seen drawings of you guys in books," Daniel said. "I'm Daniel."

Daniel and the Maccabee shook hands. "We still tell your story," Daniel said.

"How fearless and brave you were, and everything."

The Maccabee straightened his shoulders proudly. "We were brave, all right! But fearless? Are you kidding?" He gave a little snort. "Do you think I spend my day singing 'Maccabees, ho!'? Nosiree! Listen, David—"

"Daniel."

"Daniel," said the Maccabee. He did two quick push-ups, then patted the ground beside him. "Have a seat. I'll tell you a story."

"I like stories," said Daniel, sitting down.

The Maccabee leaned comfortably against the water fountain.

"When the fighting began," he said, "at first I hid in a cave with my brother and sisters. We were afraid to go out. But inside the cave it was dark and cold. We missed the rest of our family, our temple, and the sky. So one day I said to my brother, Jonah, and my sisters, Amy and Veronica—"

"Hey, those are the same—" interrupted Daniel.

"I said, 'No more hiding! We must fight for our people's freedom!' " The Maccabee waved his fist in the air.

Thump. Thump. Thump.

"Oh, no! Antiochus's elephants!" cried the Maccabee, jumping up. He had a scared look on his face. "I've got to join the others now."

"Good luck," said Daniel. Then he remembered something. "Hey, elephants love peanuts! Try giving them some! Peanuts!"

But the Maccabee was far away, a small speck running toward the hills.

"What's this about peanuts?" asked Mr. Bloom, putting his hand on Daniel's forehead. "Were you dreaming about the circus?"

"Not exactly," Daniel said.

Good thing it was just a dream, he thought. He had given the Maccabee terrible advice. If the elephants knew that the soldier had peanuts, they'd come charging right at him!

But maybe the Maccabee could hide the

peanuts in the hills. The elephants would run here and there, trying to sniff them out. And then Antiochus's troops would get lost on the way to battle. Daniel hoped he would meet that Maccabee again. Then he could tell him his peanut plan.

"Which reminds me," said Mr. Bloom, sitting down on the couch. "I remember what happened now. My best friend invited me to go to the circus. He could invite only one special friend. It was his birthday and he really wanted me to go. So I decided to keep my eyes closed whenever the clowns came out."

"But the clowns come out all the time," said Daniel.

"True. You could say I didn't really *see* the circus. I kind of listened to it."

Daniel giggled.

"Well, it was a start," said his father.

SATURDAY
Big Joe Zucchini

The next day was Saturday. A beautiful Saturday! The sun sparkled on fresh snow. The sky was blue and clear. Daniel could see his friends Sam and Lara building a snowman in the little yard in front of the apartment building. Daniel opened the living room window and leaned out.

"Hey, Daniel," called Sam. "Come help us."

"I'll be right down," said Daniel.

"Not with a fever, you won't!" said Mrs. Bloom, coming into the room.

"But, Mom!" cried Daniel. "My temperature is only ninety-nine degrees, right? Hardly any fever at all. You said so yourself."

Mrs. Bloom closed the window. "It's still a fever," she said firmly. "You want to be well for the family party on Wednesday, don't you?"

"But my throat doesn't hurt anymore. I feel fine. Watch this!" said Daniel. He did two push-ups on the living room floor.

"Excellent. But you still have to stay inside until your temperature is normal," said his mother, leaving the room. "I've got some paperwork to do now. But in a little while I'll challenge you to a game of Monopoly."

Daniel sighed. He looked out the window again. He watched Lara toss a snowball to Sam.

"Good shot," said Daniel, opening the window.

"Coming down?" Sam asked. He began rolling the snowball in the snow to make it bigger.

Daniel shook his head. "I've still got a fever."

"Too bad!" said Sam. He put the big snowball on top of the snowman. "There. That's his head."

"Daniel, I know how you can help us," said Lara. "Our snowman needs a face. Clothes, too."

"Be right back," said Daniel.

He ran to the hall closet. He found a scarf and a football helmet.

"Here," he said, tossing them out the window.

"Great," said Sam. "But he still needs a face."

"Just a minute," said Daniel. He ran into the kitchen. "Mom, where are the carrots?" he asked, peering into the refrigerator bin.

"We're all out," said his mother.

"I'll take this zucchini instead," Daniel said.

"But, Daniel," said Mrs. Bloom, "a *raw* zucchini? How about snacking on an apple?"

"A zucchini is exactly what I want," Daniel said.

In his bedroom Daniel found two gold-foil–wrapped circles of chocolate Hanukkah *gelt*. He found a piece of red yarn. He put everything into a bag. Then he ran back to the living room window.

"Here, guys, catch!" he called.

"Perfect," said Sam. He put the gold circles, the yarn, and the zucchini in the right places. "Our snowman is finished."

Lara and Sam began tossing snowballs at each other.

"Hey, let's all play football!" said Daniel. "Let's pretend the snowman is Big Joe Zucchini, the best quarterback in the league."

Lara and Sam huddled around Big Joe, who told them what to do. Daniel leaned out the window to hear the play too.

"Okay," said Lara. "Pretend I just got the ball from Joe!"

"I'm in the end zone," said Daniel. "Throw the ball to me!"

Lara threw the snowball to Daniel, hard and fast. The crowd went wild!

"I've got it! I've got it!" yelled Daniel.

But he was wrong. The snowball sailed through the window. *Splat!* It hit a lampshade, then dribbled onto the rug.

"What's going on in here?" asked Mrs. Bloom, running into the room.

"A football game," said Daniel sheepishly, straightening the lampshade.

"Oh, Daniel," said Mrs. Bloom.

Daniel ran to the kitchen. He returned with some paper towels to clean up the mess. His mother felt his forehead. "You'll get even sicker if you don't rest up," she said, closing the window.

Resting up was Boring with a capital *B,* thought Daniel. He looked out the window. Only Big Joe Zucchini remained outside. Sam and Lara had gone home. Boring. Boring. Boring.

Daniel opened the window again and

leaned out. "Hey, Zucchini! What's up?" he asked.

He remembered a ventriloquist he had seen on TV. The ventriloquist could throw his voice anywhere. Maybe he could do that too. Daniel closed his eyes and concentrated hard.

"*I'm Bored with a capital* B," said the snowman in a squeaky voice.

Mr. Bloom and Amy were coming up the walk. Amy was carrying her doll, Veronica. Quickly Daniel ducked down below the windowsill.

"*That doll sure is funny looking,*" said Big Joe Zucchini.

"She is not! Who said that?" Amy asked.

"*Over here! The guy in the football helmet,*" said the snowman. "*They call me Big Joe Zucchini.*"

"Snowmen can't talk," said Amy. "Anyway, you sound like my brother Daniel."

Daniel heard his father chuckle. And then he heard something else.

Barking. Ferocious barking.

Daniel peeked above the windowsill. That huge dog, Rusty, and a young woman were coming up the walk. The young woman almost dropped her bag of groceries as Rusty strained at his leash. He was barking loudly at Big Joe Zucchini.

"Quiet, Rusty!" said the dog's owner. Rusty stopped barking. But he glared fiercely at the snowman, growling every now and then.

That dog is a big bully, thought Daniel, who was now glad to be inside. He ducked down beneath the windowsill again.

"Sorry about the barking," the young woman was saying. "Rusty loves green vegetables. He thinks the nose on that snowman should be *his* to eat. I'm Jane. Rusty and I just moved in. We live on the second floor."

"We live on the second floor too! We're neighbors!" cried Amy happily.

Who cares? thought Daniel unhappily.

"I'm Mark Bloom," said Mr. Bloom. "This is Amy."

"This is Veronica," said Amy. "And that's Big Joe Zucchini. If he talks, it's really my brother Daniel hiding behind that window up there."

Neither Daniel nor the snowman introduced himself personally.

"Daniel must be the boy I heard having a conversation with Rusty the other day," Jane said. "I've been wanting to meet him."

"Daniel?" asked Mr. Bloom in a surprised voice.

"He fed something to Rusty that Rusty just loved. My dog's been searching for Daniel all over the second floor," said Jane.

"It couldn't have been Daniel," said Amy. "It was probably my other brother, Jonah."

"*It was Daniel,*" said the snowman. "*He fed that dog a zucchini latke.*"

Jane laughed. "Well," she said, "Rusty ate it all up. Didn't you, Rusty?"

Daniel peeked out the window again. Rusty had rolled over onto his back. Jane was tickling his big stomach.

"Veronica and I like dogs," said Amy. She tickled the dog's stomach too. "He's so cute!"

Daniel could see Rusty's long yellow teeth. Cute? *Cute?*

"Well, I've got to go home now and start my Christmas baking," said Jane.

"Do you leave out cookies for Santa?" asked Amy. "My friend Samantha does that."

"Yes. And the cookies are always gone in the morning," said Jane with a wink.

"Really!" exclaimed Amy. "Does Santa eat them?"

"*Are you kidding? That* dog *eats them,*" said Big Joe Zucchini.

Amy frowned at the snowman. "How do you know? It *could* be Santa!"

"Would you kids like to come by Tuesday, Christmas Eve, for some cookies and hot chocolate?" asked Jane. "Around seven-thirty? Rusty will show you all the neat tricks he knows."

"Jonah and I will come," Amy said. "But Daniel won't. He's afraid of dogs. He's a baby that way."

"*He is not!*" said Big Joe Zucchini. "*I bet he'll be there.*"

Oh, no! Why did you have to say that, *Joe?* thought Daniel.

SUNDAY
The Secret Present

On the fifth night of Hanukkah, Daniel received a yellow glow-in-the-dark marker pen from Jonah. He decided to use the pen to work on the gifts he was making for his family.

First Daniel cut out four big circles. Then he colored the circles with his yellow marker pen to look like Hanukkah *gelt*.

On the first circle he wrote:

Happy HANUKKAH,
Jonah Bloom!
You're a lucky guy!
I, your brother,
Daniel Bloom, will make
your bed every Monday
morning for one
month.

Daniel decorated the circle with menorah and *dreidel* stickers. He leaned back and looked with satisfaction at what he had written. Jonah hated making his bed. He would be pleased.

Next, Amy. Daniel thought for several minutes. Finally on the second circle he wrote:

I read 2 U on sunny days.

Daniel frowned. Amy's gift wasn't as good as Jonah's, he realized. Daniel usually read to Amy whenever she asked, no matter what day of the week it was. Maybe he'd come up with something better later, he thought guiltily. He still had time.

Next, his parents.

"It isn't necessary to get us Hanukkah gifts," his parents always said.

But Daniel thought it was fun to give his parents gifts. It made him feel grown up. The gifts had to be homemade, or cost less than two dollars. Those were his parents' rules. Daniel had thought about their gifts for a long time. And his father's gift was terrific, if he did say so himself.

From under his bed, Daniel pulled out a long, skinny box of plastic wrap. He wrapped the box with Hanukkah gift paper. Then he made the card on one of his big yellow circles. He wrote:

Dear Dad,
Every time you trim your mustache, put some of this over the soap first. Then Mom won't get mad at you for getting hairs on the soap.
HAPPY HANUKKAH!
Love,
Your son Daniel

Only his mother's gift was left. Daniel took a shoe box from under his bed and opened it. Inside the shoebox was a little painted piece of clay.

"What's that?" asked Jonah, wandering into the bedroom.

"Mom's gift," Daniel said.

Jonah leaned over and looked into the shoe box. "Interesting. But what is it?" he asked.

"It's a secret," said Daniel.

Actually, the present was so secret, he wasn't even sure what it was himself. It had started off as a little jewelry box when he had first shaped the clay at school. But when he'd dried it in the school kiln, one side had curled like a leaf, and the other side had flattened out. It wouldn't hold much jewelry, but he had painted it blue and white anyway. His father had told him it was a nice piece of modern art.

"Come on, tell me what it is," said Jonah.

"I told you. It's a secret," Daniel said.

Jonah leaped on Daniel. The boys rolled

on the floor. Jonah pinned Daniel's arms down.

"One more chance! Tell me?" asked Jonah.

"No way," yelled Daniel.

"Then I'll show no mercy," shouted Jonah. "You are to be tickled to death!"

Daniel pushed as hard as he could and, to his surprise, broke free. He had never been able to do *that* before. Maybe his muscles *were* getting stronger!

"What's going on in there?" called Mrs. Bloom from the kitchen.

"Nothing," said Jonah.

"Nothing," said Daniel.

"Aw, who cares what your secret present is?" said Jonah, flopping down on his bed with a book.

Daniel sighed. He cared, that was who. How can you give someone a gift when you're not sure what it is yourself? He wrapped his mother's gift anyway, decorating the package with the rest of his Hanukkah stickers. Then he went into the kitchen, where his parents were baking cookies.

"Mom, I just want to warn you," Daniel said. He paused to pop a menorah cookie into his mouth.

"Warn me about what?" asked Mrs. Bloom. She sprinkled blue and white sugar on a tray of unbaked Stars of David.

"Well," said Daniel, swallowing the last bit of cookie, "you may not think the Hanukkah present I made you is so great."

"Of course I will! It's the thought that counts, honey. You know that," said his mother. Then she put her hands on Daniel's shoulders and looked into his eyes. "I will cherish your gift always," she said.

"I hope so," Daniel said gloomily.

"Hey," said Mr. Bloom, "did I ever tell you the story about me and the potato chips?"

"No," said Daniel, perking up. He sat down at the kitchen table. Today he was in the mood to hear one of his father's stories.

Mr. Bloom poured himself a cup of coffee, then sat down beside Daniel. "When I was about your age, I loved potato chips. Still do, as you know. I got it into my head to write a thank-you note to the potato chip company for the wonderful potato chips they produced. I wrote the letter in my best handwriting and mailed it off."

Daniel liked to imagine his father as a young boy. In old photos, with no mustache, he looked sort of like Daniel.

"About a month after I wrote that letter," continued his father, "a big van pulled up to my apartment building. I happened to be looking out the window. And a driver hopped out carrying a great big can of . . . ?"

"Wow! Potato chips?"

"You guessed it. They really liked my letter. So after I ate the potato chips—took me about a week—I sat down and wrote a poem about my favorite chocolate bar. Sent that off to the chocolate bar company."

"And you got some chocolate bars?" asked Daniel.

"Half a dozen. Ate them, then sat down and wrote a letter about my favorite soda pop, and you know the rest."

"You got sodas!" said Daniel, giggling.

"Right. Then I had this brilliant idea. You see, my parents' car was in terrible shape. It needed a new carburetor and a paint job. Even its dents had dents! So I wrote a long letter to the president of the automobile company, praising his wonderful cars. And then I waited."

Mr. Bloom paused to sip his coffee.

"And?" asked Daniel impatiently.

"I waited. And I waited. Every morning I looked up and down the street, expecting to see one of those long trailers carrying my parents' shiny new car. It was this very time of year, I remember, and I figured it would make a terrific Hanukkah gift. Probably the best gift they'd ever received in their lives! And then it came."

"Wow!" said Daniel. "A car!"

"Well, no. A note from a big-shot executive at the company, thanking me for my interest in their cars. I was so disappointed, I cried. I had really believed the car would come."

Daniel nodded. He would have cried too.

"I showed the big shot's letter to my father and told him the whole story. He said the car wasn't important. He said it was the thought that counted. Of course I didn't believe him."

Mr. Bloom put his arm around Daniel. "But now I do," he said. "I really do."

"A gift of love," said Mrs. Bloom. "That's the very best gift of all."

Daniel was quiet for a few moments. "It would have been nice to get that car, though," he said.

"You're right," said Mr. Bloom, who had gone back to cutting out Hanukkah cookies. "It would have been nice."

Daniel went into his bedroom. On the fourth yellow circle he wrote:

Dear Mom,
This is a thought box.
I made it myself.
There are lots of good
thoughts in it from me to you.
(You can also put your
ring in this box when
you take it off.)
HAPPY Hanukkah!
Love,
Your son
Daniel

MONDAY
Oil, Zoil

Jonah was writing a Hanukkah poem for the big party on Wednesday. He wanted to tell the entire Hanukkah story in rhyme, he said. Daniel knew that took a lot of brain-power.

But there was a secret to rhyming. And Daniel had finally figured it out.

"Maybe you can use an assistant," Daniel said. "A rhyming assistant."

Jonah looked up from his papers. His

cheeks were flushed. His hair stuck out from the sides of his head. He had a pencil behind his ear.

"Well, okay," Jonah said. He reached for a Hanukkah cookie from the plate on his desk. "See what rhymes you come up with for 'oil' and 'miracle.' And also 'Antiochus,' if you have time."

"Easy," said Daniel.

First he got his own plate of Hanukkah cookies. Then he sharpened two pencils. He put one pencil behind his ear. He wrote out the alphabet, all twenty-six letters, just the way Jonah had. And he crossed out the vowels, *A, E, I, O, U,* also the way Jonah had. Then he wrote *oil* beside each of the alphabet letters that were left.

"Boil, coil, doil," whispered Daniel. He put a circle around *boil* and *coil.* He stopped to eat a cookie. He studied his list. "Is 'doil' a word?" he asked.

"No," said Jonah.

Daniel worked slowly. There was a lot to

think about. He ate two more cookies. Finally he came to *zoil,* but he did not put a circle around it. "Done!" he said proudly. "Well, my first list anyway."

Jonah studied Daniel's list. "You circled 'loil' and 'roil,' " he said.

"Right," said Daniel, munching on another cookie. "The Maccabees were *loil* to one another. Antiochus was a king. He was *roil.*"

Jonah giggled. He took the pencil from behind his ear and wrote *loyal* and *royal.* "You spell them like this."

"Oh," said Daniel.

Sometimes there's just too much to know! thought Daniel as he got into bed. Rhyming was harder than he'd thought. He would continue tomorrow.

Jonah climbed into his bed too. " 'Loyal' is a good word for my poem," he said. "Now think of a rhyme for 'miracle.' "

"That's a tough one," said Daniel drowsily. And then he fell asleep.

* * *

Creak, creak.

Daniel woke up suddenly. He glanced at the clock on his night table. 11:48 P.M.

Rustle, rustle.

What were those noises?

Daniel searched for his special radio, a Hanukkah present from the previous night. Attached to the radio was a handy flashlight for emergencies. He hadn't expected to use it so soon! Quietly he swung his legs over the side of the bed and felt for his slippers with his feet. He switched on the flashlight. Then he tiptoed from his bedroom.

Rustle, creak.

Daniel poked his head into the living room. A dark figure was curled up on the floor near the fireplace! Daniel's heart began to thud. A burglar? He was just about to run for his parents when—

Munch, munch.

The dark figure was chewing something! It reached toward a plate on the floor. Daniel tiptoed closer. The dark figure turned toward him and jumped up.

It wasn't a burglar at all. It was Amy.

"Who's there?" she demanded.

"It's me, silly. Daniel," Daniel answered in a loud whisper. "What are you doing?"

Amy sighed, picking up the plate from the floor. She flopped down on the couch with her doll, Veronica, on her lap. Daniel sat down too.

"Veronica and I fell asleep waiting for Santa," Amy said. She smelled like cookies.

"Christmas Eve is *tomorrow* night," said Daniel. He switched on the lamp. There were two cookies on the plate, one shaped like a *dreidel,* the other like a Star of David.

"But I wanted Santa to taste our cookies before you and Jonah ate them all up," said Amy. "I thought Santa might be out practicing in the sky tonight."

Daniel pointed to the window. "Look! There he goes!" he cried.

Amy turned her head. Quickly Daniel grabbed the Star of David cookie and hid it behind a pillow.

"Oh, sorry," he said. "It wasn't Santa. It

was a shooting star. But guess what? Santa was here already. You missed him."

"Really?" asked Amy, her eyes wide. "How do you know?"

"How many cookies did you put on the plate?" asked Daniel.

"Four," said Amy.

"How many did *you* eat?" asked Daniel.

"Two," said Amy.

"Two and two makes four, right?" Daniel pointed to the plate. "But look! There's only one cookie left. Santa ate the other one while you were sleeping."

Amy stared at the cookie. "Wow!" she cried. "Santa's probably never had Hanukkah cookies before."

"Oh, I'm sure he has," Daniel said. "Although not as good as ours, of course."

"Maybe I'll stay up again tomorrow night," Amy said.

Daniel smiled to himself. He remembered when he had been Amy's age. He had wanted to meet the real Santa too. But deep down he had always been glad *his* gifts came from his family. *What if Santa lost his way in a snowstorm one year, or a great gust of wind blew all the gifts from his sleigh?* he used to wonder. All of a sudden Daniel felt much, much older and smarter than Amy. It was a good feeling. It was probably how Jonah felt every single minute of his life.

Amy yawned and leaned against Daniel. "You know what, Daniel?" she said.

"What?" Daniel asked.

"One day maybe one of our Hanukkah gifts will be a dog," said Amy. She looked at Daniel. "Right?"

Daniel stared at his feet. He didn't say anything.

"Some dogs are nice," said Amy. "Rusty is."

Daniel shrugged. All of a sudden he didn't feel like such a big brother anymore. He remembered how Amy had hugged Rusty just that morning, when Rusty had been out for his walk with Jane. And how he, Daniel, had scampered inside the apartment building like a scared rabbit.

"Well, I guess I'll go back to bed now," Amy said. "Good night."

"Good night," said Daniel.

Wouldn't it be great if I could give Amy a dog for Hanukkah? thought Daniel. One of those tiny puppies with big floppy ears. Amy would be so happy. "This is the best Hanukkah present ever! Thank you, Daniel!" she'd say.

Except that tiny puppies grow up to be big dogs, of course. And it would take a miracle for Daniel to stop being afraid of dogs. Amy was only five. She believed in miracles. But wouldn't it be great if one could really happen?

Miracle, biracle.

Not easy to find a rhyme for it, either.

Daniel munched on the Star of David cookie slowly, point by point. Maybe he'd tell Amy that he, not Santa, had eaten the cookie.

And maybe he wouldn't.

TUESDAY
The Riddle

On the seventh night of Hanukkah, Daniel chose to open a small box wrapped in white paper with a blue bow. He hadn't really noticed that gift on the other nights. It had been hidden behind a big tin of popcorn he'd unwrapped the night before.

He opened the card first, because that was the polite thing to do. It said:

Dear Daniel,
 Here's a riddle. What is a four-letter word that begins with L? That's what

this gift will bring to you. (It used to belong to your mom.)

Hugs and kisses special delivery from California,

Grandma Ava and Grandpa Rick

Inside the box was a silver *dreidel*. Daniel spun the little top across the living room floor, then read the note to his family.

"I know the answer to that riddle," said Amy. *"L-L-L-Latkes?"*

Daniel looked at Jonah. They both laughed.

"Lunch?" asked Amy.

"It's a *four*-letter word," Jonah said.

"L-L-L-Lion?" asked Amy.

Daniel and Jonah lay down on the floor, snorting with laughter.

Amy looked as if she was going to cry. Suddenly Daniel felt bad. "It's *L-U-C-K*. That spells *luck*," he said.

"A lucky *dreidel*!" said Amy.

Daniel read the names of the Hebrew letters on the dreidel's four sides. *Nun. Gim-*

mel. He. Shin. He knew they were the first letters of the words in the sentence *Nes gadol hayah sham,* which means "a great miracle happened there."

That miracle again. A shiver went up and down Daniel's spine. He twirled the *dreidel* once more, staring at the silver blur. What if his new *dreidel* really *was* lucky, just as his grandparents had promised?

"Mom, did this *dreidel* bring you good luck?" Daniel asked.

"Absolutely," said Mrs. Bloom. She spread both arms wide. "Look how lucky I am today."

"Come on, Mom, *really,*" said Daniel.

But his mother just smiled.

"It's just a top for an old Hanukkah game," said Jonah. "It doesn't have special powers or anything."

Mr. Bloom picked up the *dreidel.* It glinted in the light of the Hanukkah candles. "I don't know about that," he said. "This little top and its games were very important in the days of the Maccabees."

"Really?" asked Daniel.

"Story time!" said Amy, plopping down on the couch.

"A short one. Dinner is almost ready," said her father. He sat down on the couch beside Amy. "We already told you how King Antiochus forbade the Jews to study the Jewish Bible. Well, some boys already knew the whole thing by heart."

"The whole thing? Wow!" said Jonah.

"They would get together to study secretly," continued Mr. Bloom. "One of the boys would be chosen as the lookout. 'Soldiers coming!' he would warn. 'Hide those books!' And out would come their spinning tops and other toys. The soldiers would be fooled, thinking the boys were playing games. They didn't guess what those boys were *really* doing!"

Sometimes he himself did just the opposite, thought Daniel guiltily. He pretended to do his homework when he was really playing on the computer.

"Who knows?" said Mr. Bloom. "Maybe

a Jewish soldier, going into battle, would think about those *dreidel* games. He would remember his friends and family at home. And he would feel strong. Maybe he would even feel lucky."

At dinner Daniel placed the *dreidel* near his plate while he ate. Did he actually feel a tingly feeling at the back of his neck? A fluttery feeling in his chest? A lucky feeling all over? Yes! Definitely.

"I challenge you guys to a *dreidel* game!" Daniel said to his sister and brother after dinner.

Jonah looked at his watch. "We said we'd go next door tonight. It's almost seven-thirty. I want to see that dog do tricks."

"Come on, just one game," Daniel begged. "I *do* feel lucky tonight! I know I'll win for sure."

And maybe, thought Daniel, *the game will be so much fun they'll forget all about going next door.*

"I'll set the kitchen timer for fifteen minutes," said Jonah. "At the end of that time we'll see who's the winner."

Daniel sighed. Jonah was just too smart for him.

"Come play with us, Amy," said Jonah. "It's more fun with three people."

Jonah brought out the timer and the bowl of chocolate *gelt*. He gave everyone seven pieces. Jonah, Daniel, and Amy sat down on the living room rug.

"Veronica wants to play too," said Amy.

"Dolls can't play!" said Daniel.

"Yes, they can," said Amy, folding her arms across her chest. "I won't play if she can't."

"Oh, let her play," said Jonah. He counted out seven pieces of *gelt* for Veronica, too. "Now I'll review the rules for you dummies who don't know them."

"That's a mean thing to say," said Daniel.

"I'm talking to the doll," said Jonah. "Okay. Everyone put one piece of *gelt* into the middle. That's the pot."

Everyone did that, including Veronica/Amy.

Jonah held up the *dreidel.* "See these Hebrew letters on the sides of the *dreidel*?"

"I see them," said Amy. "So does Veronica. Right, Veronica?"

Daniel rolled his eyes.

"When it's your turn to spin the *dreidel*," continued Jonah, "if it falls on *nun,* just do nothing. If it falls on *gimmel,* take the whole pot. *He,* take half the pot, or half plus one if it's an odd number. *Shin,* give half your own pile. And everyone puts in one piece after each person's turn."

Jonah set the timer for fifteen minutes. "The person who has the most *gelt* when it rings is the winner."

Tick, tick, tick went the timer.

Jonah spun the *dreidel.* "*Nun.* Do nothing. Oh, well. Don't forget to put one piece in the pot after each turn, everybody."

Amy spun. *Shin.*

"Give half of your pile to the pot. That's three," Daniel told her.

Veronica/Amy spun. "*He!* Take half!" shouted Amy. Daniel helped her figure out how much that was.

Daniel spun. He wished for luck. "*Gimmel!* Take the whole pot!" he cried. Daniel scooped up all the pieces.

Tick, tick, tick.

Soon Jonah, then Amy, had no *gelt* left and were out of the game. Daniel had eight pieces in his pile. Veronica had twelve. There were eight pieces in the pot.

Tick, tick, tick. The timer showed two more minutes to play.

"This is a tense moment in Bloom City, folks," said Jonah, whispering into a pretend microphone. "Two *dreidel* masters, Veronica and Daniel, fighting to win. Can Daniel make it back to the top?"

Veronica/Amy spun. *Nun.* Do nothing.

Veronica/Amy and Daniel each put one piece back into the pot.

Tick, tick, tick.

Veronica/Amy still had four pieces more than Daniel. Was a *doll* going to beat him?

He spun. *Gimmel* again! Take the whole pot!

"Yes!" Daniel shouted, scooping up the pieces.

Each player put one piece back into the pot.

Tick, tick, tick.

"Only half a minute of play left," whispered Jonah. "The pot has two. The score is Daniel, sixteen; Veronica, ten. It's not over yet, folks."

"It sure isn't!" said Amy, spinning the *dreidel* for Veronica.

He. Take half. Amy gave her doll one piece from the pot.

Brr-ing! Brr-ing! went the timer.

Daniel looked down at his *gelt.* "I won!" he cried. Grandma Ava and Grandpa Rick had been right. He had *L-U-C-K!*

"Phooey," said Amy.

"Veronica put up a good fight," said Jonah, getting up from the floor. "Time to go see that dog."

Amy brightened and jumped up too. "Are

you coming, Daniel?" she asked. "You said you would."

"Yes," said Daniel, suddenly feeling brave as well as lucky. "Of course I'm coming."

Mr. and Mrs. Bloom put down their newspapers and stared. Mr. Bloom grinned.

"Good going, Daniel," said his father. "Now, remember what we always tell you. There are two signs of a friendly dog. The ears will be down. The tail will be wagging like crazy."

Daniel looked at the lucky *dreidel* in his hand. "I'll remember, Dad. Don't worry."

"Here, take these with you for our new neighbor," said Mrs. Bloom. She gave Jonah a platter of Hanukkah cookies.

"Maccabees, hey! Maccabees, ho!" sang Daniel, marching down the hall in front of his brother and sister. "Come on, troops, let's go!"

He could hardly believe it. Here he was, going to meet a dog, and he wasn't even afraid.

Much.

Just a tiny flutter in his stomach, that was all.

Jane opened the door. "Hello!" she said. "Hanukkah cookies! Thank you. I have some cookies for you, too."

Daniel could hear Rusty barking. The tiny flutter in Daniel's stomach had grown as big as an ocean wave. His heart began to pound. His knees felt weak.

"This is Jane, guys," said Amy. "These are my brothers, Jonah and Daniel."

"Hi," said Jane.

Rusty barked again, more loudly this time. Daniel backed away from the door. He felt so ashamed! *What a baby I am, after all,* he thought. "I'm sorry," he said in a small voice. "I'm afraid of dogs. A dog bit me once."

Jane put her hand on his shoulder. "Daniel, I understand," she said. "Look, I've put a chair by the front door, just for you. We'll leave the door wide open. And Rusty is under strict orders to stay right where he is."

"Come see, Daniel! It's beautiful in here," said Amy, stepping into Jane's apartment.

From the hallway Daniel saw a brightly decorated Christmas tree. Beside the tree, wearing a red stocking cap, lay Rusty.

"Aarf!" barked Rusty. He began to get up. Daniel grabbed Jane's arm.

"Stay, Rusty," said Jane sternly. Rusty sat down again, staring mournfully at Daniel.

"He won't bother you, I promise," said Jane. "But you're the boy he's been looking for, you know. He thinks you're his friend."

"*I'll* be his friend," said Amy. "So will Veronica." She ran over to the dog. She patted Rusty's smooth, sleek coat.

Daniel noticed that the dog's ears were down. *Friendly sign number one,* thought Daniel. Slowly he entered the apartment and sat down on the chair near the door. Still, he wasn't crazy about being in the same room with the dog. Nothing had changed. He was just a big baby and always would be! Amy was only five years old, but look at her. *She* wasn't afraid, not one bit. She would love to have a dog like Rusty, more than anything.

"How about some hot chocolate and cookies?" said Jane, passing a big tray.

"Yum," said Amy, choosing a cookie shaped like a Christmas tree.

Jonah chose a candle, and Daniel a chocolate reindeer.

"Now, Rusty," said Jane, taking a cookie from the plate, "you can have a cookie, but first do your stuff. Roll over, please."

Rusty rolled over, then sat up again.

"Give me your paw," said Jane. Rusty put his big paw in her hand, looking very pleased with himself. "Good dog," said Jane.

Rusty barked at her loudly.

"Here you are," said Jane, giving him the cookie. "And now for the best trick of all." Jane picked up her camera from the coffee table. She crossed the room. "I can get Amy, Jonah, and Rusty in the picture from here. Now, smile when I give the signal. And watch Rusty carefully." Jane peered into the camera lens. "Okay, kids. Say pizza!"

"Pizza!" shouted Jonah and Amy.

"Pizza," said Daniel softly.

"Look, Rusty's smiling too!" Amy said.

From across the room Daniel leaned forward to get a better look. Rusty had stretched his mouth so that his teeth were showing!

"Good dog," said Jane, taking the picture. "All right, this is the last cookie," she said to Rusty. "No more."

The dog stared at the rest of the cookies. *Drip. Drip.* His drool made a small puddle on the rug.

"Oh, what a messy dog you are. I'll get some paper towels," said Jane, going into the kitchen.

Daniel began to reach for his mug of hot chocolate. All at once the silver *dreidel* fell from his hand. It bounced two times on the floor. Then it skittered lightly across the room, stopping at Rusty's front paws.

Rusty picked up the *dreidel* in his mouth and stared right at Daniel. Before Daniel knew it, the dog was lumbering across the room, his claws clattering loudly. Heading right toward *him*! Daniel jumped up from his chair.

"Uh-oh," said Amy.

Now Rusty was so close Daniel could see the dog's yellow teeth and the freckles on his wet nose. Daniel stiffened, staring at Rusty. He felt as if he couldn't breathe.

Rusty dropped the *dreidel* at Daniel's feet.

Daniel looked down. *Shin,* said the *dreidel.* Give half.

Thump. Thump. Was that his heart pounding? No, it was the dog's tail, thumping the floor like crazy. Friendly sign number two.

Daniel took a deep breath. Slowly he reached for his cookie. His hands shaking

just a little, he gave half of the cookie to
Rusty. The dog's big, rough tongue tickled
his fingers.

"Good dog," whispered Daniel. "Good
dog."

WEDNESDAY
A Hanukkah
Party to Remember

It was always the same, thought Daniel. You waited a whole year for Hanukkah. Then—*poof!* The holiday week was over.

He opened his bedroom window and leaned out. The snow was coming down hard. Mr. Rumper was outside, shoveling the walk.

"Merry Christmas, Mr. Rumper," called Daniel.

"Happy Hanukkah, David!" said Mr. Rumper with a wave. "They say this snow will turn to freezing rain by tonight."

"By the way, my name is Daniel," said

Daniel. "Here's a good way to remember. The first part, 'Dan,' rhymes with 'can,' 'fan,' 'man,' and 'plan.'"

Mr. Rumper made an "okay" sign with his gloved fingers. "Daniel. Thanks. I'll remember that."

Daniel shut the window and went back to his desk. He was making a new card to go with Amy's Hanukkah gift. Rhymes buzzed in his head. *Bog, cog, fog, frog.*

Jonah came into the bedroom. He flopped down on the bed. "You're not going to believe this," he said.

"Believe what?" Daniel asked absentmindedly, without looking up. He wrote on Amy's card:

A dog
Is more fun
Than a frog.

"Mom's making orange *latkes* for the party! Dad's making those green ones again. And Mom said they're even thinking of making *purple* ones!" wailed Jonah.

"I know," said Daniel. "But I think carrot and eggplant *latkes* are worth a try. We liked the zucchini ones."

Jonah held his nose. "I can't stand it!"

Something very weird was happening in the Bloom family, thought Daniel. This week Jonah was growing down. Daniel himself was growing up!

He finished the verse on Amy's card:

And you can jog
With a dog.

L _ _ _ ꜛ
↗   Your brother
        Daniel

hint: rhymes with 🖐xxx

He would help her read it. Underneath the poem, he drew a dog with brownish red fur, sort of like Rusty. There. All done. Now he would go get Amy's gift.

"Where are you going? We have to practice our Hanukkah show," said Jonah, sitting up.

"Again? We've only practiced it a zillion times," Daniel said, pausing at the doorway.

"We need to have a dress rehearsal," said Jonah.

"We'll still have time when I get back," said Daniel.

He tried not to giggle. Jonah was wearing a skirt made from an old bath towel pinned around his waist. He didn't look at all like a Maccabee soldier.

"Real Maccabees wore sandals," Daniel said. "Not sneakers."

"You're right," said Jonah, staring unhappily at his feet. "But my sandals don't fit anymore."

"Neither do mine," said Daniel.

In the kitchen Daniel breathed in the delicious cooking smells. Chicken. Brisket. *Latkes*. Probably hundreds and hundreds of them!

"May I have two of each kind of *latke*?" he asked.

"That's quite a few, don't you think?" said Mrs. Bloom.

"Don't worry. They're not for me. They're a gift." Daniel piled some *latkes* on a plate. He stretched plastic wrap over them. "Do you have some bows I can stick on top?" he asked.

"Sure. Who's the gift for?" his mother asked.

Daniel grinned at her. "For Jane and Rusty."

He went next door and rang the bell. There were turkey smells coming from Jane's apartment. He could hear music and people laughing inside.

"Well, hi!" Jane exclaimed, opening the door.

"Merry Christmas," said Daniel.

Wearing a festive green bow around his neck, Rusty barked happily. He scampered toward Daniel. Nervously Daniel took a few steps backward.

"Whoa, boy!" said Jane, grabbing Rusty's collar firmly.

"These are *latkes,*" said Daniel, giving Jane the wrapped plate. "They're for both of you. And I'm wondering if you could give me something in exchange. A dog biscuit."

Daniel described the Hanukkah card he had made for Amy. "I want to tape the dog biscuit inside the card," he said. "Sort of like a promise, you know? I figure we'll be getting our own dog soon. I'm not as scared of Rusty as I used to be. He's only one dog, but it's a start."

Jane nodded. "It's a good start. And there are other friendly dogs like Rusty."

"Zillions, probably," said Daniel.

"Hey," said Jane. "Why don't we take Rusty for a walk?"

"Right now?" asked Daniel.

"Sure. Let's go before the snow gets too deep," said Jane. "You get your coat while I find that dog biscuit."

Rusty gave a little yelp, as if he understood. As if going for a walk with Daniel and Jane was more important than anything.

Outside, the snow was falling quickly and silently. Big Joe Zucchini was now a tall, shapeless mound, still wearing his football helmet.

Jane threw a Frisbee. Rusty leaped to grab it with his teeth, then ran back. His big paws made long tracks in the fresh snow. He dropped the Frisbee at Jane's feet.

"Your turn, Daniel," said Jane.

Daniel threw the Frisbee high and far. Rusty caught it again.

"Good catch!" cried Daniel.

With the Frisbee in his mouth, Rusty raced toward Daniel. Big Joe Zucchini, that great quarterback, was speechless with amazement. Daniel felt brave and scared at

the same time, but the scared feeling was beginning to melt, like snow in the sun.

All afternoon the snow continued to fall. By dusk it had turned to freezing rain. Daniel could hear ice pellets rattling the windowpanes. He looked out the kitchen window. Cars were inching down the street.

"Of course we understand," Mr. Bloom was saying into the kitchen telephone. "There's always next year."

"What's wrong?" asked Mrs. Bloom.

"Aunt Nancy, Uncle Al, and the kids won't be coming tonight," said Mr. Bloom, filling the teakettle with water for tea. "And Aunt Judy's car got stuck in her driveway. I think we'll have to cancel the party. The streets are much too icy for safe driving."

"Oh, phooey!" said Daniel, disappointed. He had really wanted to challenge his cousins to a game of *dreidel*!

"We can still have a party," said Mrs.

Bloom. "It will just be a little smaller, that's all."

After a while the electric teakettle began whistling. Suddenly it stopped in the middle of its song. The kitchen went dark.

"There are no lights in the living room!" said Jonah, running into the kitchen.

"The electricity must be out in the whole apartment," said Mr. Bloom.

"Double phooey," said Daniel. "How can we have a party in the dark?"

Mrs. Bloom rummaged in a drawer for a flashlight and candles. Daniel ran through the darkened apartment to his bedroom. He brought back his own battery-powered radio/flashlight.

"Freezing rain has snapped power lines all over the city," a radio announcer said. *"Many areas are without electricity."*

"Will it be dark for a long, long time?" asked Amy, looking worried.

"I'm sure city employees are working hard to fix things," said Mrs. Bloom with a sigh. "I hope it doesn't take too long. All our food will spoil if we can't refrigerate it."

Daniel stared out the kitchen window. How lonely and strange the city looked now! It was pitch-black outside, except for the cars' headlights. Every now and then a candle or a flashlight's beam lit up an apartment window.

Daniel had an idea.

"Why don't we invite people in the building to come to our party?" he asked.

"Good thinking!" said Jonah, looking at Daniel with admiration. "That means a bigger audience for our Hanukkah show."

Daniel liked the idea of roaming through dark hallways with his emergency flashlight. He would pretend he was on a special mission. "Let's go knock on some doors, guys!" he said to Jonah and Amy.

Mr. Bloom picked up the telephone receiver. "You don't have to do that. The phones are working. Luckily *those* power lines are underground," he said. "Let's see who can come."

The young couple and their baby from the third floor came. So did Mr. and Mrs. Ezra, from down the hall. They brought *latkes,* a big salad, and their menorah. Lara brought her menorah, too. She also brought her parents and grandparents and a big bag of jelly doughnuts, called *sufganiyot.*

Then Mr. Rumper arrived with his two visiting grandsons. Daniel hadn't even known he was a grandfather.

"Hi, Nathaniel," said Mr. Rumper with a wink. "Just kidding. I mean Daniel, of course."

Daniel winked back at him. Maybe Mr. Rumper hadn't remembered his name. But Daniel himself didn't know much about Mr. Rumper, either. Except that he was good at shoveling walks.

Soon Jane arrived. She was carrying a turkey on a platter and had her camera around her neck. With her were three friends, her brother, her aunt, and her parents.

And Rusty. "Arrf!" he barked, scampering to Daniel. Daniel leaned down to scratch behind Rusty's ear.

"Well," said Mr. Bloom softly, "look at that."

"Daniel!" exclaimed Amy.

Daniel grinned at his sister. She was going to love his little present. In a million, zillion years he couldn't have thought of a better one.

"Welcome, everybody," said Mrs. Bloom. "Come and gather around. Let's light all these menorahs!"

All the candles on all the menorahs were lit and the blessing sung. The glow lit up the room. Shadows danced on the walls.

"Oh, how lovely," said Jane, snapping a picture.

"Please take your seats, everyone," said Daniel. "It's time for our Hanukkah show."

Jonah stepped forward and began.

*"The Hanukkah lights are not to keep
you warm,*

*They are not to bring light when there's
a very bad storm,
They don't do any work as they shine so
bright,
They just remind us of the wonders of
another night."*

"And now, ladies and gentlemen," said Daniel. "We bring you the candle that does all the work—the *Shammes* Candle!"

Amy stepped forward. Her red hair glowed in the candlelight.

"I light the candles from left to right," Amy began. She held up her right arm, then her left.

"Left arm first," whispered Daniel.

"I light the candles from left to right," repeated Amy, holding up her left arm first, then her right. "Every single Hanukkah night!"

Amy bowed. Everyone clapped and Rusty barked. Jane snapped a picture.

Jonah came forward again. "We now bring you the Two Maccabee Brothers!"

Jonah stepped backward into the shadows. He came forward again, with Daniel at his side. Jonah began:

"We will tell you a story and you will say,
'What a wonderful story you've told us
    today!'
Does the name 'Antiochus' ring a bell?
Well, he's part of the story we will now
    tell!"

And Daniel continued:

"It's the Hanukkah tale, it's not too long,
About a troop of fighters, brave and
strong,
Mattathias and Judah, all the Maccabees
    loyal,
And the rededication of the temple with
    the miracle oil."

Then Jonah and Daniel took turns reading the story from *The Happy Hanukkah Holiday Book*. Daniel gazed at the audience as Jonah read. So what if he and Jonah and Amy were wearing bath towels and sneakers? You couldn't really tell by candlelight. A sudden shiver went up and down his spine.

This is just how it was in the days of the Maccabees! he thought. No electricity. No TV. No radios or computers. Just family and friends, singing and praying and telling stories together. Helping each other feel brave when the night was dark and cold. Or when their enemies came.

And so what if he and Jonah hadn't had time to figure out the whole Hanukkah story in rhyme?

Shiver.

Wasn't it a miracle that they were still telling the story, thousands of years later?

Daniel and Jonah bowed deeply. Rusty barked as the audience clapped. Jane snapped another picture.

"Bravo!" called Mr. Rumper.

Mr. and Mrs. Bloom began carrying out platters of food.

"Just one more picture before we sit down to eat," said Jane. "Gather 'round, everybody!"

"Too bad they didn't have cameras in ancient times," said Jonah. "Somebody could have taken photos of that eight-day miracle oil to prove it really happened."

Jane focused the camera. "Say pizza!" she said.

"Pizza!" everyone shouted.

"Zucchini!" said Daniel joyfully.

And Rusty smiled.

That night Daniel dreamt about the Maccabee again. The two of them swapped stories under an olive tree.

"Well, I've got to go now," said the Maccabee-in-the-dream. He did two deep-knee bends, then retied his sandals. "Wish me good *L-U-C-K.*"

"Good luck," said Daniel-in-the-dream. "It was great to meet you."

"Great to meet you, too," said the Maccabee. "Tell me, does this story turn out all right in the end?"

"Well, yes," said Daniel, happy to share what he knew.

"Oh, good!" said the Maccabee, looking relieved. He stood straight and tall. "Actually, I'm not that surprised." He patted a little cloth purse hanging from his belt. "Got my peanuts for the elephants right here. Thanks for the idea."

"Before you go," said Daniel, "let me tell you my new peanut plan."

latke recipes

POTATO LATKES

Ask an adult to help you with this recipe. It requires grating by hand (or the use of a food processor if you have one) as well as frying in hot oil.

4 potatoes, peeled
1 large onion
3 eggs
¼ cup flour
1 teaspoon salt
freshly ground black pepper
pinch of baking soda
vegetable oil
sour cream and applesauce

1. Grate the potatoes by hand or in a food processor, then grate the onion.
2. Insert the steel blade in the processor and add the eggs, flour, salt, pepper, and soda. Pulse just until mixed. (If you do not own a food processor, add the eggs, flour, salt, pepper, and soda by hand and mix well.)

3. In a large skillet, heat ¼ inch of oil. The oil must be very hot. (You can use two skillets and fry two batches at once, for speed!)

4. Spoon large tablespoonfuls of potato batter into the hot oil, flattening with the back of the spoon. Brown, turning *only once*.

5. Drain on paper towels. (You can keep the *latkes* in a warm oven as you fry the remaining batter.)

6. Serve with sour cream and applesauce.

Makes 2½ to 3 dozen latkes.

Two Make-Ahead Tips

• You can prepare the batter a few hours ahead, cover with a thin layer of flour, and refrigerate. Remove the flour with a spoon before frying.

• You can freeze *latkes*. They'll still taste wonderful, though not extraordinary.

This recipe by Joanne Rocklin has previously appeared in Writers in the Kitchen, *compiled by Tricia Gardella, Boyds Mills Press, Honesdale, Pennsylvania, 1998.*

MIRACLE ZUCCHINI LATKES
(they use hardly any oil!)

Ask an adult to help you with this recipe. It requires grating by hand (or the use of a food processor if you have one) as well as baking in a hot oven.

5 **medium zucchini, unpeeled**
3 **scallions, sliced**
2 **eggs**
²/₃ **cup seasoned bread crumbs (or more**
   if needed, up to 1 cup)
salt and pepper to taste
vegetable oil

1. Preheat the oven to 425 degrees.
2. Clean the zucchini well. Grate by hand or in batches in a food processor. Lay out the zucchini on layers of ink-free paper towels; cover with more paper towels. Let stand for half an hour.
3. Place the zucchini in a bowl and mix with the other ingredients (except the oil). Use your hands to make a "dough" that sticks together.
4. Pour about 1 tablespoon of oil on each cookie sheet (you will need two sheets). Spread the oil with a paper towel.

5. Mound the zucchini mixture on the cookie sheets with a tablespoon. Press down with a fork to make pancakes about 2½ inches wide.

6. Bake for about 12 minutes, or until the pancakes turn brown on the bottom (not the top). Turn the pancakes over and bake for an additional 5 minutes.

Makes 18 to 20 small latkes.

From Melting Pot Memories, *by Judy Kancigor, G & R Publishing Co., Waverly, Iowa, 1999.*

About the Author

JOANNE ROCKLIN is the acclaimed author of more than a dozen books for children. A former elementary-school teacher and psychologist, she now writes full-time. She is a member of the Advisory Committee for the Museum of Tolerance "Once Upon a World" Storytelling Program of the Simon Wiesenthal Center in Los Angeles and is a founding member of the outreach organization California Readers. Originally from Montreal, Joanne Rocklin has two grown sons and lives in Los Angeles with her husband, Gerry, and three cats.

About the Illustrator

CATHARINE O'NEILL, who has illustrated numerous picture books and children's novels, lives in Ithaca, New York, with her partner, daughter, and dogs.

EVERY SECRET LEADS TO ANOTHER

SECRETS *of the* MANOR

W9-BNC-378

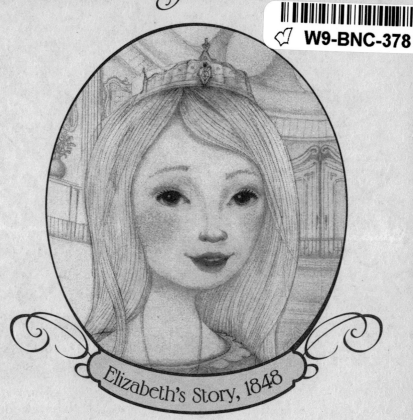

Elizabeth's Story, 1848

BY
ADELE WHITBY

Simon Spotlight

New York   London   Toronto   Sydney   New Delhi

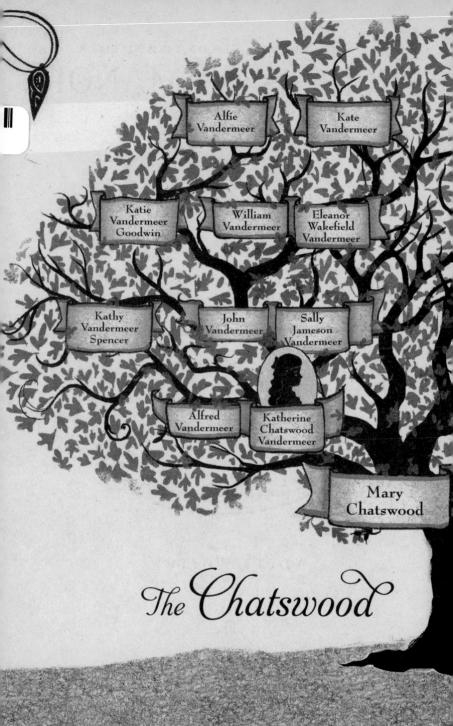

Alfie
Vandermeer

Kate
Vandermeer

Katie
Vandermeer
Goodwin

William
Vandermeer

Eleanor
Wakefield
Vandermeer

Kathy
Vandermeer
Spencer

John
Vandermeer

Sally
Jameson
Vandermeer

Alfred
Vandermeer

Katherine
Chatswood
Vandermeer

Mary
Chatswood

The Chatswood

Beth Etheridge

Gabrielle Trufant

Liz Burns Etheridge

Edwin Etheridge

Beatrice Etheridge Trufant

Claude Trufant

Eliza Tynne Burns

Douglas Burns

Edward Etheridge

Charlotte Gordon Etheridge

Elizabeth Chatswood Tynne

Maxwell Tynne

Cecily Smith Etheridge

George Etheridge

Robert Chatswood

Family Tree

SIMON SPOTLIGHT
An imprint of Simon & Schuster Children's Publishing Division
1230 Avenue of the Americas, New York, New York 10020
This Simon Spotlight paperback edition August 2014
Copyright © 2014 by Simon & Schuster, Inc. Text by Laurie Calkhoven.
Illustrations by Jaime Zollars. All rights reserved, including the right of reproduction in whole or in part in any form. SIMON SPOTLIGHT and colophon are registered trademarks of Simon & Schuster, Inc. For information about special discounts for bulk purchases, please contact Simon & Schuster Special Sales at 1-866-506-1949 or business@simonandschuster.com.
Designed by Laura Roode. The text of this book was set in Adobe Caslon Pro.
Manufactured in the United States of America 0514 OFF
2 4 6 8 10 9 7 5 3 1
ISBN 978-1-4814-1841-6 (hc)
ISBN 978-1-4814-1840-9 (pbk)
ISBN 978-1-4814-1842-3 (eBook)
Library of Congress Catalog Card Number 2013953184

$\mathcal{I}$ rolled over and stretched, enjoying the coziness of my silk down comforter. A housemaid had already been in to build up my fire, the gentle warmth it gave off welcome on these chilly June mornings. I could almost hear the house, Chatswood Manor, waking with me, ready to greet another day.

I knew that downstairs, servants were going about their morning routines, quietly bustling about, opening curtains, building fires, dusting, and cleaning. Our cook, Mrs. Fields, was no doubt scolding the kitchen maids to work more efficiently to whip eggs or slice bread for our breakfast, and Mr. Fellows, the butler, would be instructing the footmen on their tasks for the day before reading the newspaper and finishing his own breakfast in the servants' dining room. Mr. Fellows made a point of talking to Papa about the news of the day every morning when he served our meal in the family dining room.

Early morning was my favorite time of day. For a few moments every morning, when my mind was no longer asleep but not quite fully awake, I could almost forget that Mama had died just a few weeks ago.

But then, as always, I remembered. That now-familiar sinking feeling crept into my chest and settled in my heart. Next came the sting of tears behind my eyelids.

I sat up and reached for the silken bellpull that would call my lady's maid, Essie Bridges.

I promised myself that I would stop this, I thought, wiping my eyes. *And more important, I promised Katherine. We made a vow to be strong for each other, and for Papa.*

It was as if Katherine, my twin, could read my thoughts. At that moment, she walked through the dressing closet that connected our two bedchambers and leaned against the wall, a sleepy half smile on her face. Her eyes, too, had a trace of tears.

Katherine and I were so nearly identical that only Mama could tell us apart in an instant. The only obvious physical difference between us was in our hair: Katherine's had a lovely natural wave while mine was stick straight. I envied Katherine that wave she had in her hair, while Katherine envied the fact that I was a half inch taller than she and five minutes older. I teased her that I would gladly give her my half inch in height if she would give me her wavy hair.

"I just heard Papa's valet in the hall instructing Mrs. Cosgrove to meet us in the library after breakfast. We're going to discuss the guest list for the birthday ball," Katherine said. "We'd better ring for Essie."

"I was just about to," I said, reaching again for the bellpull. The pull was connected to a bell in the servants' hall downstairs, where our ladies' maid, Essie, would hear it and come to our aid. Essie had been with Katherine and me since we were very young. We loved her dearly. It was Essie who helped to dry our tears after Mama died and Essie who always knew just what to say when we were feeling down or scared. She wasn't a blood relative, of course, but she was as much family to us as we were to each other.

I can still remember the first time Katherine and I met Essie. Essie has told me that I was too little to really remember all of these details, but I swear I do! Katherine and I were puzzling over the alphabet in the nursery, trying to put our blocks in the correct order, when Essie came in, a bright smile on her pretty face. Immediately, I knew that she was different from all of the other servants I was used to seeing. There was something very special about her. She crouched down next to us and told us her name was Essie Bridges and that she was going to help take very good care of us. Then she attempted to help us with our letters, but as it turned out, she didn't know them either. Later, after Katherine and I were taught to read and write by our tutors, we taught what we had learned to Essie. She resisted at first, telling us it wasn't a good use of her time and that our parents weren't paying her to learn; they were paying her to care for us. But Katherine and I insisted! We kept after her until she relented. It didn't seem right to us that Essie couldn't enjoy reading books as we could. She was a quick study—I daresay she learned even more easily than Katherine and I had. But then again, perhaps she had better teachers!

While we waited for Essie this morning, Katherine plopped onto my bed to talk about our birthday, which was just over two weeks away. We had had parties before, of course, but for our twelfth birthday, Papa was throwing us a true birthday ball with more guests than we could count, a full orchestra, and beautiful custom-made dresses to wear. We had even been taking lessons with a dancing master.

This party was going to be the most spectacular social event of the season, perhaps even the year! In getting ready for the ball, it was as if Papa's estate, Chatswood Manor, and all of its inhabitants were shrugging off our sadness about Mama and beginning to live again.

"I can't wait to waltz with someone other than Mr. Wentworth," Katherine said.

We were giggling and whispering about dancing with boys when we heard a quiet knock on the door.

"Come in, Essie," I called.

"Good morning, Lady Elizabeth. Good morning, Lady Katherine," Essie said, walking quickly into the room and smiling at us as she did each and every morning. "What are you girls giggling about?" she asked us in a mock-serious voice.

"Nothing!" Katherine and I said in unison.

5

"Now, I'm quite sure I don't believe that!" Essie replied, her grin widening. "Something tells me you were whispering and giggling about your party! Am I right?"

Katherine and I nodded. "We're going over the guest list with Papa and Mrs. Cosgrove after breakfast this morning," I added.

"I've a list of questions for you from Mrs. Fields and Mrs. Cosgrove," Essie replied, digging through the pockets of her apron until she found a small piece of paper. "We can go through some of them while I get you girls dressed and ready for the day. Beginning with what kinds of flowers you'd like."

"Blue hydrangeas," Katherine said.

"Red roses," I announced at the same time.

Then we laughed. Katherine's favorite color was blue and mine was red. Of course we each wanted the flowers to be in our own favorite color.

Essie laughed along with us as she opened the doors to my armoire. She was used to us saying opposite things. It happened almost as often as we said exactly the same thing! Essie liked to say that she never knew what to expect from us.

I figured that made us exciting to be around!

"What would you like to wear today, Lady Elizabeth?" Essie asked. I had worn almost nothing but black over the past several weeks, but yesterday Katherine and I asked Essie to pack our black dresses away. It was time to bring color back into our lives. It's what Mama would want.

I pointed to a purple day dress, still not ready to wear anything too brightly colored. "That one," I said.

Essie laid the dress across my red chair, and I suddenly remembered a lesson about colors that my art teacher had shared some time ago. "Red and blue combined make purple," I said to Katherine. "What if we decorate the ballroom with purple flowers?"

"Splendid idea!" Katherine cried. "Violets and pansies are purple," she mused. "I love those."

"And hyacinth and irises, too," I added.

"There's a good compromise, then," Essie said. "I love it when you girls work together to solve problems."

"It probably won't be so easy to compromise on a cake," Katherine replied teasingly as she headed into her own room to choose a dress.

I held my arms up for Essie to pull my silk

nightgown over my head and then stepped into my underclothes and my petticoats before she carefully lowered the purple dress over my head and shoulders.

While Essie fastened the buttons that ran the length of my back and tied my sash, I pinned my chatelaine to the front of my dress. I wore the silver brooch always. The charms attached to it chimed like little bells—a notebook and pencil, a paint box, and a tiny tear catcher.

It was good to be wearing something other than black. I felt the familiar tug on my heart, remembering Mama, but I shook it off and thought about something happier—cake.

"How about an all chocolate cake?" I shouted to Katherine.

"Lady Elizabeth, it's not ladylike to shout," Essie reminded me.

"Sorry, Essie," I said in a much more appropriate tone.

"You always want all chocolate," Katherine shouted back. "I want a lemon cake with Mrs. Fields's creamy ivory frosting."

Instead of yelling back and upsetting Essie with

my unladylike behavior, I followed the sound of my sister's voice. A wonderful idea had formed in my mind. Essie trailed behind me, brushing my hair and pulling it back from my face with pretty silver combs.

"Two cakes!" I announced when I reached my twin's bedchamber. "A chocolate cake for me and a lemon cake for you."

"That idea might be even more splendid than your idea about purple flowers!" Katherine exclaimed. Then her brow furrowed. "But do you think Mrs. Fields will mind? Two cakes is twice as much work."

I hadn't thought of that, but Katherine was right. Was it fair to ask Mrs. Fields to bake not one but two birthday cakes for us? Was it dreadful of me to even have suggested it?

As if sensing my panic, Essie smiled at me reassuringly. "I agree it's a splendid idea!" she said brightly. "You turn twelve only once! I think Mrs. Fields will be happy to make as many cakes as you'd like."

"Oh, Essie, do you really think so?" Katherine asked.

Essie nodded. "I'm sure of it. It brings her such pleasure to make you girls happy. She'll be pleased to see you smiling again after everything you've been through these past months. . . ." Essie's voice trailed off and she cleared her throat. She didn't have to finish. We knew what she meant.

We were all quiet for a moment, remembering Mama. Seeing the tears forming in Katherine's eyes, I quickly changed the subject. "Do you know if all the responses have arrived?" I asked Essie.

"I know that Lord and Lady Tynne have sent word that they'll be here, along with your cousin Maxwell, of course."

At the mention of Cousin Maxwell, Katherine and I both began to giggle.

"I had a feeling that was one reply you'd be happy to hear of," Essie said with a smile. "He is a handsome young man; I'll give you that," she said.

"I wonder if he's gotten even more handsome—and taller—than when we saw him last," Katherine said. She turned her back to us so that Essie could fasten her buttons, but not before I saw a hint of pink washing over her cheeks.

"Handsome?" I asked, considering Cousin Maxwell's looks. "Maybe a little, but I think Edward Smythe is even more handsome. And Charles Clarkson as well." I twirled on my tiptoes like a ballerina. "I want to dance with *all* the boys," I announced.

Katherine burst into giggles again. We hadn't done very much dancing with boys, at least not yet.

Essie didn't share our giggles this time. "It's best you remember that one day Lord Maxwell will be your husband, Lady Elizabeth."

I wrinkled my nose.

"He'll inherit this house and become the Earl of Chatswood himself one day," Essie reminded me.

It was true. By law, Papa's title and estate would be inherited by his closest male heir, and that was my thirteen-year-old cousin, Maxwell. It was Papa's and Mama's dearest wish that their eldest daughter would marry him one day. Being five minutes older than Katherine made me the eldest daughter. I sometimes thought it was a pity that Katherine wasn't born first. She seemed to think it romantic and exciting that it had been decreed I would one day marry Maxwell. I wasn't sure how I felt about it. Maxwell was a perfectly fine young man, but I thought it would be more exciting and romantic to wonder about whom my husband might turn out to be.

Katherine and I had made many plans over the years about what kind of man *she* would marry. Sometimes I suggested she marry a sea captain or the son of a mysterious foreign count. Other times we plotted to marry her off to Prince Albert, even though he was a few years younger than we were, so she would one day be Queen of England.

"You'll have to curtsy when you greet me and call me Your Majesty," she had said, laughing.

"And you can make me the very first female knight," I had responded.

Mostly we wanted to be sure that whoever he was, her husband's estate would be near enough to Chatswood Manor to allow us to visit whenever we had a fancy to do so. I couldn't imagine not seeing my dear twin sister every single day! Katherine felt exactly the same way.

"I know I'll marry Maxwell one day," I told Essie with a sigh. "But that's ages and ages away. First I want to do lots and lots of dancing, with lots and lots of boys."

As soon as Katherine's dress was fastened and her

hair done, we went to join Papa for breakfast. No one was about, so I ran down the stairs, something that would have drawn a frown from Mr. Fellows. Our butler was more of a stickler for proper behavior than even Papa was, and now that Katherine and I were young ladies, we were told that it was more becoming to walk than to run. Still, sometimes I just couldn't help myself.

We joined Papa at the table and exchanged good mornings while Thomas, one of the footmen, poured our tea. A moment later he came to our sides with a platter of eggs and sausage, from which we served ourselves. A plate of hot buttered toast sat on the table, along with a bowl of Mrs. Fields's delicious marmalade.

Mr. Fellows came in with the morning's post and a letter opener on a silver tray. There was an air of excitement in his normally dignified and measured step as he leaned down to whisper in Papa's ear.

Papa's eyes flashed, and he took up the envelope on the top of the pile. "Girls, this is exciting news," Papa said. "Buckingham Palace has responded to your birthday invitation."

I gasped. "Queen Victoria?"

"Is she coming to our ball?" Katherine asked, her voice a high squeak.

"Let's see," Papa said, opening the envelope.

I could tell that Mr. Fellows was doing his utmost not to read over Papa's shoulder.

"Her Royal Highness Queen Victoria congratulates Lady Elizabeth and Lady Katherine on the occasion of their twelfth birthday," Papa read. "The queen finds herself unable to travel so soon after the birth of Princess Louise but thanks you for the invitation."

I sat back with a sigh of relief. "I'm sure I'd be terrified if the queen came to Chatswood Manor," I said.

"Me too," Katherine agreed.

Papa smiled at us and then eyed Mr. Fellows. Our butler seemed more than a little disappointed.

"Fellows, you'd like a visit from the queen, I think," Papa said.

Mr. Fellows nodded in his dignified way. "A visit from Her Majesty would bring great honor to Chatswood Manor," he said.

Papa laughed. "And a great deal of terror to the young ladies within."

After breakfast we met with our housekeeper, Mrs. Cosgrove, in the library to go over the rest of the guest list for the ball. First we talked about the flowers, and she promised to discuss our desire with the head gardener. Then we shared our idea about the cakes.

"Two cakes?" Papa asked. "Isn't that a lot of work for Mrs. Fields on top of everything else?"

"Oh, she might have a bit of a grumble, milord," Mrs. Cosgrove said. "But we're bringing in two girls from the village to assist the kitchen staff, and that will be a tremendous help. I'll talk to her right after I see the gardener and will let you know if she anticipates any problems, but I think this is a request she'll be happy to fulfill."

Papa nodded. "And now the guest list," he said.

We went over the long list of Papa's friends and

family relations. Nearly everyone we invited—everyone except the queen, thank goodness—had written that they would come. Katherine and I exchanged a happy glance when we heard that both the Smythes and the Clarksons would be attending, along with their sons.

"Two more boys to dance with," I whispered as soon as we left the library. "I was afraid that I'd have to spend the whole evening dancing with old uncles and friends of Papa."

"Don't forget Cousin Maxwell," Katherine said, her cheeks turning pink again.

"Let's go down to the kitchen and talk to Mrs. Fields ourselves about the cakes," I said. "She surely won't say no to us directly, even if she would grumble to Mrs. Cosgrove."

"Just make sure that Mr. Fellows doesn't catch us," my sister said in a nervous voice. "You know how upset he gets if we try to venture downstairs! Our being belowstairs upsets all his feelings of dignity and decorum."

I sometimes thought Katherine would never break a rule if it weren't for me always being right next to her, urging her to do so once in a while. I pushed open the door that led from the great hall to the servants' area. The stairs were empty. "Let's go."

"I'm going to ask for blue rosettes and pearls on my cake," Katherine whispered, her concerns about getting caught forgotten already

I tiptoed behind her. "And I'll have red rosettes with matching pearls on mine," I said.

We stepped into the hall. Mr. Fellows, Mrs. Fields, and Essie were talking to a thin, shabbily dressed man in the servants' dining room. He nervously twisted a battered hat around and around in his hands. Although it was obvious to anyone that Mr. Fellows was the person in charge, the man's eyes and his words were focused on Essie's much more friendly face.

Katherine sucked in her breath sharply as soon as she spotted Mr. Fellows and turned to head back upstairs before we could be seen, but something about the man caught my interest. I put my hand on her arm and held my finger to my lips to let her know to be quiet. We lurked just outside the servants' hall, listening.

"Her name is Maggie O'Brien," the man said in a

thick Irish brogue. "And she came here to work as a scullery maid in 1827."

Mrs. Fields shook her head. "That's two years before my time," she said. "I'm sorry, but I can't help you."

"It's been more than twenty years since she was employed here?" Mr. Fellows interrupted. His tone was indignant. "And you're just beginning to look for her now?"

"Circumstances kept me away from England," the man said, his voice full of sorrow. "I was in India for many years. When I stopped getting Maggie's letters, I wanted to return to look for her, but I didn't have the means to do so. When I finally made it home again, I went directly to Ireland, and Maggie's family told me that they hadn't heard from her in that time either."

"I have no memory of such a maid," Mr. Fellows said. From his tone, I had the impression he didn't believe what the man was telling him.

"Please," the man pleaded. "It was her dear mother's dying wish that I find her. She doesn't believe Maggie ran off."

Mr. Fellows shook his head. "She's not employed here now. Of that I can assure you."

"Were you butler here in 1827?" the man asked.

Mr. Fellows pulled himself up to his full height. It was his most dignified pose. "I was first footman, under butler William Adams," he said.

Mr. O'Brien started to ask another question, but Mr. Fellows cut him off. "I can assure you that Chatswood Manor has never been a home for abandoned wives. Now, I must ask you to leave here at once."

"Please, Mr. Fellows," Essie said. "Can we not give the man a bite to eat first? He looks like he could use it, and I'm sure it's what Lord Chatswood would want us to do."

"Very well," Mr. Fellows said with a frown. I could tell he didn't like Essie's suggestion that she knew better than he did about what Papa would want.

He turned back to the man with an icy stare. "But you are to leave directly afterward."

The man nodded, and Mr. Fellows swept out of the room. I pulled Katherine back against the wall, but the butler didn't even look in our direction. He went into his office and closed the door with a loud bang.

"Come, Mrs. Fields," Essie said. "I'll help you fix a plate and pour the tea." She turned to Mr. O'Brien with a friendly smile. "Have a seat. I'll be back in a moment."

I couldn't help but wonder about the poor man who was trying so hard to find his wife. Where could she have gone? People don't just disappear, never to be heard from again! I had to know more! As soon as Essie and Mrs. Fields had entered the kitchen, I tugged Katherine toward the servants' dining room.

"Papa won't like it," she said, trying to hold me back.

"Papa won't find out unless you tell him," I answered in my most practical voice. "And besides, this is a mystery, just like in the books we read! There could be a real-life mystery unfolding around us. Do you really want to miss out on this?"

I could tell I had convinced Katherine from the way her eyes sparkled with excitement.

The man jumped to his feet when we entered and started twisting his hat in his hands again.

"Please do sit down," I said. "And tell us all about your wife. Don't leave out a single detail!"

If the man was wondering how we knew of his missing wife, he didn't show it. He just looked nervous.

"It's all right, really," I assured the man. "My sister and I live here, and we want to hear all about your wife. Perhaps we can help you find her!"

The man still looked a little unsure, but I think he couldn't resist the chance to talk to someone about his wife. "My name is Sean, Sean O'Brien," he stammered. "And my wife is Maggie."

"What can you tell us about Maggie, Mr. O'Brien?" I asked.

When he began to talk about his Maggie, there seemed to be a candle shining in Sean O'Brien's eyes. He told us about how Maggie could read and that her dearest wish was to become a teacher.

"She just needed a bit more schooling first," he said. "Not many girls in Ireland learn to read. Nor boys either. Maggie wanted to change that. She was a fine teacher. She even taught me to read, and believe you me, I wasn't an easy one to teach!"

I nodded, remembering how even Essie didn't know how to read when she came to work for us, though she had been a wonderfully easy pupil to teach.

"Shortly after we married, I had a chance to work for the East India Trading Company—in India," he said. "Oh, how I hated to leave my Maggie. But it was a grand chance to make good money. Money to send Maggie to teacher's school and to make our dreams come true." Mr. O'Brien shook his head with a regretful air. "We both agreed it was the right thing to do, and we came up with a plan. I was going to make my fortune and come home to Maggie or send for her. Maggie got a job here as a scullery maid while she waited. She kept our marriage a secret—married women weren't taken into service. She hated to lie, of course, but it couldn't be helped. Besides, it wasn't the sort of lie that would hurt anyone."

I nodded sympathetically.

"And then what happened?" I asked.

Sean O'Brien was about to answer when he jumped to his feet again.

I turned to see Essie, a tray of food in her hands. "Ladies," she said with alarm. "What are you doing in here? Lord Chatswood would be very displeased, and Mr. Fellows would have my head."

"Oh, please, Essie," I said. "We were talking to Mr. O'Brien here about his missing wife. We simply must help him to find her!"

"We have to hear the rest of his story," Katherine added. She patted the cushion next to her. "Please sit and listen too. We simply must help if we can—don't you agree it's the right thing to do?"

Essie could never resist when we pleaded. She shook her head with a sigh and took a seat next to Katherine. "Be quick with it then," she said nervously.

Mr. O'Brien, whose eyes darted from the food to Essie's face and back again, seemed relieved when she relented.

"Please sit," I told him. "Eat your meal and tell us the rest of the story."

Mr. O'Brien took a few bites and then continued. "As soon as I had the money to send for her, I did so. But before that, Maggie's letters had stopped coming and Maggie herself never came to India. I wanted to come back to search for her, but I had some reversals and it took me years to save enough money again to sail for Ireland."

"There was no trace of Maggie there?" I asked.

"I searched and searched. I spent every penny I had. No one had heard from her since the autumn of 1827, just a few months after we parted. Even I began to believe what everyone else did, that Maggie had run off with another man and didn't want to be found," Mr. O'Brien admitted. "I told myself I had let her down when I failed to become wealthy and successful in India, and she had moved on to a better life without me. I tried to move on too, but I never stopped loving my Maggie, or wondering what had become of her." His voice grew thick, and I feared he was going to cry. He took a moment to compose himself and then continued. "But then, just a few weeks ago, her dear mother called me to her bed as she was dying of the hunger. She told me that she knew deep in her heart that Maggie would have never left me for another man. She told me she knew Maggie loved me with all her heart. She begged me to take up looking for Maggie again. I promised her I would. And so I came here."

"Do you think she's living in England still?" Katherine asked.

Mr. O'Brien shook his head. "I believe my Maggie is in heaven with her ma, but I need to find out what happened to her."

"Has the hunger been very bad?" Essie asked quietly.

The hunger. That was the second time we had heard that phrase now. Mr. O'Brien must have seen the question in my eyes.

"The potato crop has failed us three years in a row now," Mr. O'Brien said.

I was confused. Why would it matter if the potato crop had failed in Ireland? There were lots of other things to eat besides potatoes.

"Most of the Irish live on potatoes," Essie explained. "The crop failures have been devastating to the people there." She turned to Mr. O'Brien. "I have family in Ireland. I pray for them every day."

"Perhaps your prayers are working," he answered. "Things have been very bad. Many people have died, and many others have sailed for America, but this year's crop looks strong—so far, anyway. If we can get through these next few hungry months, things will be greatly improved come August."

"I am glad to hear that," Essie told him.

I couldn't believe what I was hearing. People had died from not having enough food to eat? My eyes filled with tears, and I saw that Katherine was just as upset as I was. How did we not know that so many people were hungry? There must be something we could do to help. I resolved to put the question to Papa.

Mr. O'Brien finished his meal and got to his feet. "Well, I'll be on my way. I'm much obliged to you," he said to Essie. "And to you young ladies. It was nice to have someone listen while I talked about my Maggie. I believe she is no longer here, of course. I wish there was some way to know what happened to her after she left, but I understand that it was a very long time ago."

"I'm sorry I couldn't help you find your Maggie," Essie said.

"But surely you can do *something*," I said to Essie. "Some of the other servants might have information. What if someone remembers Maggie?"

"You must try to find out," Katherine urged.

Essie hesitated for a moment and then agreed. "I'll make some inquiries," she said. "Come back in a week's time and I'll tell you what I've discovered. But don't get your hopes up," she said. "It's unlikely I'll find out anything of use."

Mr. O'Brien nodded. His eyes shone in excitement and appreciation.

"May I ask your name?" he asked Essie suddenly.

"Essie," she answered. "Essie Bridges."

Mr. O'Brien's eyes widened and he stared at Essie intently, as if he was trying to commit her face to memory. Then he lowered his gaze. "Thank you for your kindness," he said. "I haven't known such a kind-hearted lass since my Maggie."

We walked Mr. O'Brien to the door to the servants' yard and watched him leave. We were asking Essie about which of the maids might have been at Chatswood at the same time as Maggie when a stern voice made us jump.

"Lady Elizabeth. Lady Katherine," Mr. Fellows said. "What brings you to the servants' hall?"

"We came to talk to Mrs. Fields about our birthday cakes," I answered quickly.

"And is Mrs. Fields outside?" he asked, looking at Mr. O'Brien through the window in the door.

I could only shake my head. I didn't have a fast answer for that one.

"You're young ladies now, not children," Mr. Fellows said. "Old enough to ring the bell for myself or Essie when you'd like to speak to one of the staff. I'm sure that's what Lord Chatswood would prefer."

He gave Essie a pointed look. "I do hope you haven't involved Lady Elizabeth and Lady Katherine in the lies of a charlatan."

I was tempted to argue and defend poor Mr. O'Brien. He wasn't a charlatan! But I was afraid of getting Essie into trouble, so I bit my lip and only said, "Please tell Mrs. Fields we'd like to discuss our birthday cakes now. We will go wait upstairs for her to join us."

I took Katherine's hand and we walked to the stairs leading to the great hall.

"Mr. Fellows or not," I whispered to her, "we have to do everything we can to help Sean O'Brien find out what happened to his Maggie."

3

*L*ater that afternoon, after French lessons with our tutor and a session with Mr. Wentworth, our dancing master, Mr. Fellows rang the dressing gong to let the family know it was time to get ready for dinner. Although it was just Papa and Katherine and me for dinner, we still observed the formalities. Papa would wear his tails, as always, and Katherine and I would change into more formal evening dresses, with Essie's help.

Katherine had dressed first, and she wandered into my room while Essie helped me step into a lovely rose-colored silk dress with a flounced skirt and embroidered flowers on the sleeves and around the neckline. Katherine wore blue with tiny seed pearls forming a flower pattern on the bodice and on her sleeves. Together we looked like a spring garden, and

I hoped that would make Papa happy. He tried to hide his sadness, but I knew he missed Mama terribly. Maybe even more than we did.

I looked in the mirror while Essie fastened my buttons, still thinking about Sean O'Brien's sad story. I remembered what Essie had said about praying for the people in Ireland.

"Essie, I didn't know you had family in Ireland," I said. "Bridges isn't an Irish name, is it?"

Essie shook her head. "No, it's an English name. I don't know the name of my Irish family. Only that my mother was Irish."

Our family tree went back generations and generations. Their portraits hung on the wall and their names were listed in *Burke's Peerage*, a guide to England's landed gentry. I couldn't imagine not knowing their names.

"Mrs. Bridges was Irish?" Katherine asked.

"Mrs. Bridges wasn't my real mother," Essie replied, meeting our eyes in the mirror. "She treated me like her very own daughter though. So did my father. They were wonderful parents to me."

Katherine perched on one of my chairs, and I sat at

my dressing table while Essie did my hair and told the rest of her story.

"My real mother showed up at the village midwife's one day on the verge of having a baby—me. The poor thing died minutes after I was born. Mrs. Thornton, the midwife, knew the Bridgeses wanted a child, and so she brought me to them. I'm very lucky that they agreed to take me in and raise me as their own. I couldn't have asked for finer, more loving parents. They treated me like their very own until the day they died. I miss them dearly."

We knew that Essie's parents had died, of course. When Mama died, Essie told Katherine and me that she knew a bit about what we were feeling because she had lost both of her parents. But we had never known before now that there was even more to her story. "But that's so sad about your natural mother," I said. "Didn't Mrs. Thornton tell the Bridgeses her name?"

Essie shook her head. "Mrs. Thornton knew only three things about my mother. The first was that she was Irish. Second that she loved her unborn baby more than anything in the world and couldn't wait to hold me in her arms. And third, that if her baby was a girl, she planned to name her Essie. It was the woman's favorite name in the world."

"And the Bridgeses honored your mother's wish," Katherine said.

"They did," Essie answered, her eyes a bit misty.

"Didn't anyone make any inquiries about the woman?" I asked.

Essie shrugged. "My mother told Mrs. Thornton that she was married, but the midwife didn't believe her. No one ever came looking for her, so I think the midwife must have been correct. I have always wondered about my real family in Ireland."

My hair finished, I stood up and gave Essie a hug. Katherine joined us, and Essie's eyes filled with tears again, just for a moment.

"I'm sure you'll find out more about her one day," I said.

"As am I," Katherine added.

"It seems unlikely now," Essie answered. "It all happened more than twenty years ago. But I am proud to be Irish. One day I hope to go to Ireland to see the land my mother came from, and I pray every night that my family will survive this terrible famine, even if I never discover who they are."

I felt sad for Essie. I know she said the Bridgeses were wonderful parents, but not to know the name of your mama must be a terrible thing. I was so grateful for my own mama, even though she was taken from us too soon.

"I'm going to talk to Papa about the hunger at dinner tonight," I told Essie.

"I know he'll want to do something to help," Katherine added. "Maybe we'll even be helping your own family."

Later at dinner we did just that. I expected Papa to be as surprised about the hungry people in Ireland as Katherine and I had been, but he knew all about the famine.

"Parliament has the matter well in hand," he said. "England has sent corn to make up for the lack of potatoes. There are soup kitchens all over Ireland to help feed the hungry people. The landlords are funding workhouses, and they're even paying the fares for the Irish who want to try their luck in America."

"But, Papa, people are dying of hunger," Katherine said. "Surely there must be something we can do to help."

"You're exaggerating, my dear," Papa said. "Of course some people have died, but from old age and disease. Everyone in Ireland who wants to work for their food has an opportunity to do so."

What Papa was telling us was quite different from what we had heard from Sean O'Brien. Who was right? What was really happening in Ireland?

There were platters of uneaten food on our sideboard. After our soup course, we had been served braised salmon and green beans, followed by a roasted spring chicken and zucchini. The platters were nearly full when the footmen took them from the dining room and brought in dessert, fresh fruit, and charlotte russe.

"What will happen to the food we don't eat?' I asked Papa. "Does it just get thrown away?"

Papa sighed. "I'm sure Mrs. Fields and Mrs. Cosgrove have things well in hand."

"But—"

"Let's put an end to the matter, shall we?" Papa said.

He had made a request, but his tone was clear. The discussion was over.

In the drawing room after dinner, Katherine and I settled on the settee while Papa attended to his correspondence. We each held a book, but we were only pretending to read. In truth we were whispering about the people of Ireland. Katherine felt the same as I did, that it was confusing the way there was so much conflicting information, but if even part of what Mr. O'Brien had told us was true, we had to do something to help. The tricky part was going to be doing it on the sly.

"Mrs. Fields keeps a sharp eye on the food supply, and I've never seen her without her keys at her waist," I said. "If only she would set them down now and again, we might be able to sneak into the pantry or the larder."

"And Mr. Fellows has already scolded us for being in the servants' hall," Katherine said. "If he catches us in the pantry, he'll surely tell Papa."

"I don't want to make Papa angry," I said. "Especially after he told us to drop the whole subject. We'll simply have to take extra food ourselves at meals—a little at a time so that it won't be missed," I decided. "And when we have enough, we can send it to a family in Ireland."

I was pleased with this plan until my very practical twin raised a very practical question.

"How will we send it?" Katherine asked.

"We'll put the matter to Sean O'Brien when he returns next week," I said. "He'll know how to manage things."

Katherine nodded and then sighed. "I do hope Essie can find out something about his wife."

"He's like a storybook knight on a romantic quest, searching for his damsel," I whispered.

"What if his Maggie is really Mrs. Fields, and she was only pretending not to know him?" Katherine giggled. "Maybe she prefers bossing scullery maids about to having a husband."

"Or she could be Mrs. Cosgrove," I said, giggling along with her. It was nearly impossible to imagine Mrs. Cosgrove as young and in love.

"Mrs. Cosgrove is from Devonshire, not Ireland," Katherine whispered. "I've heard her speak of it."

"And Mrs. Fields's first name isn't Maggie. It's Gwen," I whispered back.

"Or so she says," Katherine answered, wiggling her eyebrows and giggling even harder.

Papa looked up from his letter. "How many birth-day secrets do you girls have?"

"We're only talking about the dancing, Papa," I said, lowering my book. "I do hope you're ready to waltz with each of us at least once."

"Not to worry," Papa said with a smile. "I think my old bones remember the steps. And there will be young men to dance with after you've finished with your poor old Papa."

"Oh, Papa," I said, running over to give him a kiss on his cheek. "I could never be finished with you."

"Nor could I," Katherine said, joining us and kissing his other cheek.

"You are good girls," he said. "Now, off to bed, and try to keep the whispers and the giggles to a minimum. You need your sleep."

"Yes, Papa," we answered in unison.

I turned to Mr. Fellows, who, as always, stood at the ready to help with anything we needed. "Could you let Essie know we've gone up, Mr. Fellows?"

"At once, milady," he answered and then nodded to one of the footmen.

While Mr. Fellows's back was turned, I took a biscuit

from a silver tray on one of the side tables and, grateful that my dress had pockets, slipped it inside. Katherine, seeing me, did the same. Our plan to send food to the people of Ireland had just been set in motion!

The gaslight candelabra in the great hall lit our way to the staircase and up the stairs to the second level.

Katherine entered my room with me. A cheerful fire burned.

"Where shall we hide the food?" I asked. "If Essie finds out, she might give us away to Papa. I'm sure she would agree with our decision to help, but she wouldn't want to go against Papa's wishes."

"In the corner of the dressing closet," Katherine answered after considering for a moment. "She goes in there only to find clothes that aren't in our armoires, or to walk from room to room."

"That's a wonderful idea," I said.

There was a wooden trunk in the corner of the room that made the perfect table, and we each deposited our biscuits.

"It's a small start," Katherine said.

"But it *is* a start." I was imagining a cache of food large enough to fill the trunk.

I was startled out of my reverie by Essie. "Lady Elizabeth? Lady Katherine?" she called. She had entered Katherine's room first and was nearing the dressing closet.

Katherine and I dashed into my room.

"Whatever were you two doing in there?" Essie asked.

Katherine's eyes darted from Essie to me.

"Only wondering where our riding habits were," I stammered. "We thought we might ride Star and Cricket tomorrow, so we were looking through our dressing closet."

"Tomorrow?" Essie asked. "I think you'll be much too busy with lessons and your dress fittings."

"Oh, I did forget that Madame Dubois was coming tomorrow," I said quickly. "We'll have to ride the ponies another day."

"And whenever you need your riding habits—or anything else—you need only ask," Essie answered with a quizzical expression. She frowned a little bit as she regarded us further. "You don't have to go searching through the closets, girls. You know I know where everything is! Why wouldn't you just ask me?"

My eyes met Katherine's, and I willed her think of something to say. It was no wonder Essie was looking at us like that—it was very unlike us to go rifling through our closets when Essie always fetched whatever we needed from there. Would she figure out we were up to something so soon after we began?

Katherine jumped in and changed the subject. "Have you been writing in the journal we gave you, Essie?" she asked.

Essie gave us one more long look, and then the puzzled expression on her face softened into a smile. "I have, milady," she answered, helping me out of my dress and into my nightgown. "It was hard at first to write on those beautiful pages in my own messy hand, but I write a sentence or two when I can."

"Do you ever write about us?" I asked, wanting to keep her talking.

"Oh my, Mr. Fellows would show me to the door if he thought I was writing down the secrets of the house."

"So you never write about us at all?" Katherine prodded.

Essie looked around, as if she thought Mr. Fellows might be listening in. "Sometimes I do," she said quietly.

"You are the most important people in my life, so sometimes I must. But I've given you code names in case my journal falls into someone else's hands."

"Code names," I exclaimed. "How exciting! That's like something out of a novel in Papa's library! What are they?"

My toilette finished, Essie led us toward the dressing closet and Katherine's room.

"Oh, do tell us," Katherine urged.

Essie looked around again and then, still in the dressing closet, leaned in with a whisper. "It must be our secret, girls! Do you promise to keep it?"

"Yes!" Katherine and I exclaimed together.

"Lark and Sparrow," Essie replied.

"Am I Sparrow?" I asked.

Essie nodded.

"That makes me Lark," Katherine said.

The nicknames made perfect sense, of course. Essie had named us after birds of the same shade as our very favorite colors, red for me and blue for Katherine.

Essie pulled us into a hug. Katherine reached for my hand and squeezed it. It felt so good to be embraced by our wonderful Essie.

"Don't forget. This must be our secret," Essie said. "Now, let's get you ready for bed."

When Katherine was ready, I crawled under the covers with her.

"Just for a few minutes," Essie said, turning off the gaslights. She set one candle aflame on Katherine's nightstand. "You both need your sleep."

I nodded and wished her good night, watching her walk through the dressing closet into my room, where she would do the same.

"How sad it is that Essie never got to know her mama," Katherine whispered.

"I cherish my memories of our mama," I answered. I could feel the tears pushing against my eyelids. One escaped and rolled down my cheek.

I thought Katherine might not notice. I didn't want to set her to crying too. But my twin knew what I was thinking and feeling. Katherine reached out and took my hand once again, her own voice thick with tears.

"I'm so glad we have reminders of Mama. When I look at them, it sometimes feels as if she's near," she said.

"Do you still have her trinket box?" I asked.

Katherine nodded and slipped out of bed to get Mama's mahogany box. The gold inlay on the top gleamed in the candlelight, and I could remember the box sitting on the desk in Mama's parlor.

The box was filled with things that Katherine and I loved to play with when we were little—hairpins, buttons, old keys, single earrings that had lost their mate. Whenever the servants found something while cleaning, they'd bring it to Mama, and into the box it would go until someone came to claim it. Mostly whatever it was stayed in the box.

Katherine picked up a silk button that had been painted red.

"Do you remember when you first decided red was your favorite color?" she asked. "You left the nursery with your paints and brushes and tried to make all of your clothes red."

I laughed at the memory. "I was discovered before I had time to paint more than a few buttons. They were all replaced, but Mama kept this one."

"She used to smile when she came across it," Katherine said with a yawn. "Just think . . . when you're the lady of Chatswood Manor, married to Maxwell

Tynne, the servants will bring *you* the trinkets they find."

"I wonder if the queen has a trinket box," I said. "When you marry Prince Albert, you'll have to inquire."

Katherine's giggle was interrupted by another big yawn, soon matched by one of my own.

"Time for sleep," I said, kissing her on the cheek. I slipped out of her bed and ran through the dressing closet to my own. I left the doors open, as was our habit. Then, on the count of three, we each blew out the candles on our nightstands.

"Sweet dreams," we called in unison.

Seconds later, I had drifted off to sleep.

4

After breakfast the next morning, our dressmaker, Madame Dubois, was due to arrive for our next-to-last dress fitting. I took advantage of our free hour to work with my paints—I was in the middle of creating a canvas of our spring gardens—while Katherine wrote in her journal. She was writing a story about a secret fairyland in that very same garden.

"I wish Madame Dubois didn't seem like she was going to burst into tears every time she looked at us," I said.

Katherine looked up from her story. "It is quite upsetting, isn't it? I suppose it's because she misses Mama so much."

Madame Dubois had been Mama's favorite. The two of them could go over fabrics and dress patterns for hours.

"We mustn't let her make us sad today," I said.

Katherine agreed. "We'll think of only happy things—like how elegant we'll look at our birthday ball."

I nodded. I was in the middle of adding a brilliant blue sky to my painting. "At least she's not coming at teatime today. We won't have to make conversation while she sighs and wipes her tears."

"And eats every last tea sandwich," Katherine said with a laugh.

I laughed too. Madame Dubois did enjoy her food. But not today. Coming so soon after breakfast, she wouldn't expect to be fed.

But suddenly it occurred to me that we were missing an opportunity. "Tea sandwiches!" I cried. "Let's ask Mrs. Cosgrove to provide a hearty tea. We can add whatever Madame Dubois doesn't eat to our cache of food for Ireland."

"That's a brilliant idea!" Katherine said.

I rang for Mrs. Cosgrove and relayed our request.

"So soon after breakfast, milady?" she asked. "Do you think it's really necessary?"

"Oh, yes," I said, nodding earnestly.

"The dressmaker is rather famous for her large appetite," Katherine added.

Mrs. Cosgrove couldn't argue with that. "Of course, Lady Elizabeth, Lady Katherine. I'll let Cook know."

With that settled, I put away my paints while Katherine finished her chapter, and we left the drawing room to wait for the dressmaker in my bedchamber. We came upon Essie getting a rather sharp scolding from Mr. Fellows in the great hall.

"That will be the end of the matter, Essie," Mr. Fellows snapped. "I have a delivery to attend to."

"But, Mr. Fellows, Sean O'Brien—"

"An end to the matter," he repeated. "Chatswood Manor will become the target of every charlatan in England and Ireland if we allow his storytelling to continue."

"But that's just it, Mr. Fellows," Essie said. "I don't believe he is a charlatan."

"If you want to remain employed here, you will drop this nonsense. Am I understood?"

Essie spotted us and gave a quick shake of her head, letting us know not to try to intervene.

"Am I understood?" Mr. Fellows asked again.

Essie lowered her gaze. "Yes, Mr. Fellows."

As soon as the door to the servants' hall closed behind him, Katherine and I ran to Essie to find out what had happened.

"Not here," she whispered, looking about. She led us upstairs and then filled us in on what had caused Mr. Fellows to scold her so.

"I asked him if I could look at the staff ledger to see if Maggie O'Brien did indeed work at Chatswood Manor twenty years ago. He flatly refused. He's convinced that Sean O'Brien is a liar and up to no good," she said sadly.

"I believed Sean O'Brien," I told her.

"So did I," Katherine added.

"Whether we believe him or not, that's the end of the matter," Essie said. "You heard Mr. Fellows. I'll lose my position if I keep making inquiries."

I couldn't believe Mr. Fellows could be so hardhearted. "Speak to Papa," I urged Essie. "He won't refuse you when he hears Mr. O'Brien's story. I'm sure of it."

Essie didn't look convinced, but our conversation was interrupted by the arrival of Mrs. Cosgrove with Madame Dubois.

"Tea will be up shortly," she said.

"Tea? At ten o'clock?" Madame asked.

"Yes, of course," I said enthusiastically. "We're hungry."

"Be careful of the dresses, please, ladies," Madame Dubois fretted. "Mustn't stain them before the big night."

Mrs. Cosgrove gave us another curious glance, but said nothing more about the tea.

"Now would be the perfect time to go talk to Papa," I urged Essie while Madame Dubois had her back to us.

"Yes," Katherine said. "Mr. Fellows will be busy with the deliveries for the party. Now's the perfect time."

Essie looked from Katherine to me, and we both nodded encouragingly. "All right, then," she said finally. When Essie had left, Madame Dubois began to remove our ball gowns from their muslin coverings. The last time I had seen them, they had not yet been stitched together, and now I gasped.

"Beautiful," I said, reaching to touch the white silk organza. My dress had red lace and embroidery while

Katherine's had blue. The necklines were just slightly off the shoulder, and each dress had a small train. The full hoop skirt had three flounces. I couldn't wait to waltz around the ballroom, feeling it twirl around me like a cloud.

Madame Dubois helped Katherine and me out of our day dresses and then lifted the gown with blue accents and motioned for me to step forward. I wasn't surprised. She never could tell us apart.

"That's Lady Katherine's dress," I said, stepping back.

"I am sorry, milady," she said.

Katherine stepped forward and let the dressmaker slip the dress over her head. She turned to me with a shy smile while Madame fastened the buttons up her back.

"You look beautiful and elegant," I said. "Like a grown-up."

Katherine beamed at me. "You will, too," she said, climbing onto a low stool. The dress fit perfectly. The only thing left to do was the hem.

Madame Dubois carefully pinned Katherine's hem and then began to work on mine. I felt beautiful, too, like a young lady, not a child. "You've outdone yourself, Madame," I said.

She stood back and admired her work, then raised her eyes to my hair, which was already slipping out of its combs.

"Have you decided on your hairstyle for the ball?" she asked.

"We're still trying out different things," Katherine said.

"Lady Katherine can wear lovely side curls to frame her face," I said. "But my own curls fall flat five minutes after Essie fixes them."

"Perhaps you can wear different hairstyles," Madame Dubois said. "To help your guests tell you apart."

We discussed the merits of one hairstyle over the other while Madame helped us out of our ball gowns and back into our day dresses. No one had yet touched the tea tray on the table by the fireplace, but I could see Madame's eyes drifting in that direction as she finished her work and made arrangements to return two days before the party for our final fittings.

It was rather rude of me, but as soon as I was

dressed and our ball gowns were back in their protective muslin, I led her to the door. I didn't want those tea sandwiches and scones to disappear! I wanted to send them to Ireland.

"You can see yourself out, can't you, Madame?" I said. "Lady Katherine and I have quite a bit to do to prepare for the big day."

With a last, longing look at the tea tray, the confused dressmaker stepped into the hall. A housemaid happened to be walking by, and I asked her to show Madame out.

"Of course, milady," she said. "Follow me, Madame."

Essie arrived at just that moment. Her face was flushed and she appeared upset, but I thought it had something to do with not getting back in time to see us in our dresses.

"Don't worry, Essie. You'll see us in our ball gowns on the night of the party," I said. "Did Papa show you the ledger?" I asked.

Essie shook her head and looked at the floor.

"But whyever not?" Katherine asked.

"Mr. Fellows spoke to him first," Essie said. "And

told Lord Chatswood that Mr. O'Brien was merely trying to play us for fools."

"But he didn't ask for money!" I said with feeling. "He didn't even ask for food, although he looked to be starving."

"Essie, did you explain all of this to Papa?" Katherine asked.

"Lord Chatswood said Mr. O'Brien was a beggar," Essie said, her cheeks red, "hoping to gain some advantage with his story. He was not pleased with me for coming to him, and I daresay I let him down. I should not have disobeyed Mr. Fellows. I have to let the matter rest, girls. I'm so sorry to disappoint you, and Sean O'Brien, too, but I cannot pursue this any further."

I couldn't believe that Papa wouldn't even *try* to help. He clearly didn't understand what was really happening. I wouldn't let the matter rest there—I couldn't. "There must be something we can do," I insisted. "Can you ask some of the older servants if they remember Maggie O'Brien?" I asked.

"If Mr. Fellows finds out, he'll have my job," Essie answered, shaking her head.

"We won't let that happen," Katherine told her.

Essie wasn't convinced.

"Please," I said. "There may be someone who remembers and knows what happened to Maggie. And don't forget, we promised Sean O'Brien!"

I could tell Essie wanted to help Mr. O'Brien as much as we did. It was written all over her face. But the fear of losing her job was too great. My mind was spinning. I thought if I could just find the right words, I could convince Essie to keep trying.

But then Katherine spoke up, her voice soft but firm.

"Elizabeth, it's not fair for us to put Essie in this position. She's risking her job. It's easy for us to tell her not to worry, but think about it from her perspective."

My sister was right.

"I'm sorry we pushed you so hard, Essie," I said as I reached over to give her a gentle hug. "I don't know what we would do if you ever lost your position, though I know deep down in my heart that could never happen. Papa knows how much we love you."

Katherine joined our hug, and Essie patted both of

our backs. "Thanks for understanding, girls. I really am sorry to let you down."

"You're not letting us down," Katherine said, and I nodded. We meant it. Essie could never let us down.

"I wish there was something *we* could to," Katherine said to me while Essie busied herself picking up some pins that Madame Dubois had left behind. "But if Mr. Fellows catches us talking to the servants, he'll report us to Papa, and that could cause problems for Essie."

"There is something," I said, suddenly remembering. "I know where Papa keeps the staff ledger. It's in his private library. I've seen him hand it over to Mr. Fellows many times. We'll slip in and borrow it when Papa goes out." In my excitement, I spoke loudly and Essie heard me.

"No, Lady Elizabeth," she said. "You must stay out of it as well. Doing *anything* more will bring a heap of trouble on all of us."

I glanced at Katherine, who looked as torn as I felt.

"Promise me, Lady Elizabeth," Essie said, "there will be no sneaking about."

I nodded, but only because Essie was so frightened and I couldn't bear to see her worry.

"Promise?" Essie asked again.

"Yes," I answered, but I was careful not to use the word "promise." *I'm going to get a good look at that ledger, no matter what*, I thought. *And if I am caught, I will make sure Essie isn't blamed.*

"Well, then," Essie said, surveying the room. "I think I found all the pins, so I'll just take that tea tray back down to the kitchen."

"Oh no," Katherine said, plopping into a chair next to the table. "We're hungry!"

"Famished," I added.

"As you wish, ladies," Essie said. "Try not to ruin your appetites for luncheon with your father."

As soon as Essie had left the room, we wrapped the tea cakes, scones, and dried fruit in napkins and squirreled everything away in the dressing closet. Katherine added a piece of toast she had slipped into her pocket at breakfast.

My sister looked me in the eye. "I saw you cross your fingers when you told Essie you would leave Papa's ledger alone. Tell me how you plan to get your hands on it."

I woke up the next morning still thinking about Sean O'Brien. Today was the day he was due to return to Chatswood Manor, and we had yet to discover anything about his Maggie.

That meant getting my hands on the staff ledger in Papa's private library as soon as possible. I was still wondering how when Papa let us know over breakfast that he would be going to London the next day.

I eyed Katherine, and she gave me a subtle nod. It was the perfect opportunity to slip into Papa's study and have a look at the ledger. If I could prove to Papa and to Mr. Fellows that Maggie O'Brien did indeed work at Chatswood Manor in 1827, then they would *have* to make some inquiries about what had happened to her.

"Will you be taking Mr. Fellows with you?" I asked Papa. My mission would be much easier with our watchful butler out of the house, so I hoped Papa would choose to bring Mr. Fellows along.

Mr. Fellows stepped up, ready to do anything Papa asked. "Shall I have the house opened, milord?"

Papa had a lovely house in London. We lived there during the London social season.

"No, Fellows. I'll stay at my club. It's just for one night. I'll be back on the first train the next morning. My valet will be sufficient help."

Sneaking into the office was going to be much more difficult, but it couldn't be helped. No matter what, I was going to get a look at that ledger.

*A*fter breakfast, Katherine and I went upstairs to add to the growing pile of food in our dressing closet. Katherine had slipped two apricots into her pocket, and I added another piece of toast.

Essie joined us there, wondering why we were upstairs instead of in the drawing room or taking a walk on the grounds, as we often did after breakfast.

"I forgot my book," I said, grabbing one off my nightstand.

In truth, I had finished that particular volume two days before.

"What time is Mr. O'Brien coming today?" Katherine asked.

"After the servants' lunch," Essie answered. "I hope to give the man another bite to eat along with the bad news."

"We'd like to be with you when you tell him," Katherine said.

"No, milady, you mustn't," Essie said. "I'll be in even more trouble than I already am if Mr. Fellows or Lord Chatswood were to find out."

"We won't tell them," I said.

"But I will have to," Essie answered firmly. "Your papa told me to leave this matter alone. I can't go against his wishes."

I sighed, but agreed. I didn't want to get Essie into trouble.

"Find us directly after you speak to him," Katherine said. "Please, Essie."

"Of course, milady," Essie answered.

Katherine and I whispered about Essie's meeting with Sean O'Brien whenever we had a free moment. I couldn't bear the thought of Essie sending the poor man away with no hope when I was just one day away of sneaking a peek at the ledger.

"We have to speak to him and let him know we haven't given up," I explained to Katherine for what felt like the one hundredth time.

But Katherine argued that it was too risky. "What if we're caught? What if we put Essie's job in jeopardy?" she asked.

"What if we meet with him *after* Essie has delivered her news, so she has nothing at all to do with it? No one can blame a lady's maid if two young ladies happen to run into a man on the grounds," I said. "Surely we could convince Papa of that *if* we were caught . . . and that's a big if, Katherine," I reminded her.

Finally, Katherine agreed. After luncheon we told Papa we intended to take a long walk so that we would be fit for a night of dancing—our birthday ball was just a week away.

The servants had their own luncheon directly after ours, so we were able to escape the house unnoticed. After a stroll through the gardens, Katherine and I just happened to find ourselves within view of the servants' yard.

Mr. O'Brien arrived early and stood in the yard, twisting his hat in his hand just as he had done the week before. A few minutes later, Essie joined him. We were too far away to hear the conversation, but Essie kept shaking her head. Poor Mr. O'Brien stared at his shoes, looking completely downcast.

Their talk concluded, Mr. O'Brien turned to leave. Essie placed her hand on his arm for a moment and said something more before rushing toward the house.

Essie must be going back into the house for food, I realized. I seized the opportunity. Pulling Katherine along with me, we rushed toward Mr. O'Brien. His sad expression brightened when he saw us, and he bowed with a smile.

"Good day, ladies," he said.

I knew I didn't have much time, so I dispensed with the niceties. "We're going to help you," I told him. "We're going to get our hands on the staff ledger somehow and see what we can discover."

"We have to be careful," Katherine added. "If Mr. Fellows gets wind of our plan, we'll all be in trouble. But we know it's worth the risk."

"How can we get word to you?" I asked him.

Mr. O'Brien looked from my sister to me and back again. I could tell he was overwhelmed and perhaps a bit confused as to why we were helping him. "I'll come back again this day next week," he said finally.

"No, make it the day after," I told him. "That's the

day of our birthday ball. We won't be able to slip away."

Mr. O'Brien agreed. "And I can't thank you enough for trying to help me. I do hope you'll have some good news for me."

"We hope so too," I answered. "Now we must go, before we are discovered."

It didn't matter that running was unladylike. Katherine and I quickly dashed around the side of the house just in time. Seconds later Essie rushed out of the kitchen with a basket of food and pressed it into Mr. O'Brien's hand. There was a shadow in the doorway—Mr. Fellows watched to make sure that Mr. O'Brien went on his way.

That night, just before bed, Katherine reminded me that in our hurry, we never asked Mr. O'Brien about sending food to Ireland.

"We'll have to remember next week," I said. "Let's keep saving what we can in the meantime."

I added a dinner roll to our stockpile. Our small stash was rather messy. I straightened it up a bit and Katherine laid down a piece of cheese and some fruit from dessert.

"We've got quite the cache," she said. "It'll make a lovely gift for a hungry family."

I agreed. "It will, as long as we find a way to get it to them."

"We will. Sean O'Brien will know how."

Essie came in then to help us undress for bed. She didn't seem surprised to find us in the dressing closet again. In fact, she hardly noticed. Our Essie was definitely preoccupied.

"What is it, Essie?" I asked.

She shook her head as if shaking away bad thoughts. "It's nothing, milady. Only that Mr. O'Brien was so sad when I sent him away. I believe we were his last hope of discovering what happened to his poor wife, and I feel so bad about letting him down."

I put my hand on her shoulder. "It *is* very sad," I said. "But you did everything you could to help him, Essie. And besides, I believe he'll find a clue quite soon."

"You've a kind heart, milady," Essie said. "And you too, Lady Katherine. I believe you are two of the best young ladies in England."

I felt a twinge when she said that. I hated lying to

her, but it was best she didn't know what Katherine and I were up to. There was simply too much at stake, and we had to protect Essie.

The next morning, Papa left quite early. Katherine and I had a quiet breakfast on our own, waited on by Mr. Fellows.

"And what plans do you young ladies have for today?" Mr. Fellows asked.

Katherine choked on her scrambled eggs, her pink cheeks practically giving away the fact that we had something secret planned.

I did my best to appear calm and collected. "We thought we'd read in the library," I said. "Some of our birthday guests might want to discuss literature, and we want to be prepared."

"And what do you propose to read today?" Mr. Fellows asked.

I wasn't ready with an answer, but I quickly came up with just the right title. "*Oliver Twist* by Mr. Dickens," I said. "Isn't it wonderful how he takes up for the poor?"

If Mr. Fellows made a connection between young Oliver Twist and Mr. O'Brien, he didn't let on. "Indeed,

Lady Elizabeth," he said with a nod. "You use your time wisely."

I looked at Katherine, my eyes flashing. Indeed I intended to use my time wisely. In the work of a moment, we might solve the mystery of Maggie O'Brien!

Papa's private library was just off the main library. Katherine and I went there directly after breakfast, expecting to have enough time on our own to locate the staff ledger and quickly leave.

Perhaps Mr. Fellows suspected we were up to something. First he arrived to help us locate Papa's copy of *Oliver Twist*; then he sent a footman in to see if we required anything. The footman was followed by a series of maids who arrived to fluff pillows, see if we wanted the shutters opened or closed, needed a fire, or desired Mrs. Cosgrove or Mrs. Fields to come and discuss the birthday ball.

We took turns reading aloud and were all the way to chapter three before we had a few minutes alone. I darted toward the doors to Papa's library. At just that moment, Mr. Fellows arrived to place the morning's post on Papa's desk.

"Is there something you need, milady?" he asked.

"No, Mr. Fellows," I answered. "I'm merely taking a turn around the room while Katherine reads."

"Very good, milady. I'll be just outside if you change your mind."

Just outside? We'd never get a look at that ledger if Mr. Fellows insisted on being present every moment. I had to think of a reason to send him away for a few moments.

"Has all the wine for the birthday ball been selected?" I asked. "I overheard Papa say something last night about wanting a full accounting."

Mr. Fellows seemed startled for a moment. "His Lordship said nothing to me last night or this morning when I saw him off to the train," he said.

"I'm sure it slipped his mind," I told him. "Perhaps you can prepare a list and present it to him when he returns."

"Yes, milady," Mr. Fellows said, rushing off. "Thomas is just outside, if you need anything. Or you can ring the bell for Essie."

I felt terrible. Now I had lied to both Essie *and* Mr. Fellows. I reminded myself it was for a good cause, but

I worried that neither of them would ever trust me again if they caught me in a lie.

I watched Mr. Fellows close the library doors behind him and whispered to Katherine, "I'm going to try again. Keep reading."

"I don't think you should," Katherine said nervously. "Another servant could come in at any moment, and we have no good reason to be in Papa's private library."

She was right. Even Mama hadn't ever entered Papa's study without an invitation, and Mr. Fellows didn't let the maids clean the room without his supervision. If anyone found us in the library, they would surely tell Papa.

But I had to try. I had promised Mr. O'Brien.

"Keep reading," I told Katherine. "If you hear someone coming, say, 'Oh, poor Oliver Twist. Poor, poor Oliver Twist.'"

Katherine nodded and took the chair closest to the doors leading into the library from the great hall. It was the best place to hear if anyone was coming. Once she was in position, I ran to the doors to Papa's private sanctuary.

I could hear the nervous tremor in Katherine's voice

as she read, but I couldn't focus on the words. I slipped into Papa's office. The ledger was just where I had seen it before, on the shelf above his desk. I kneeled on the desk chair to reach for it. Suddenly, the chair swiveled and the book came crashing down, hitting the desk.

I froze, expecting a footman to run in to see what had happened. There was a catch in Katherine's voice, but she continued to read from Mr. Dickens's story about the orphan boy who is forced to become a thief on the streets of London.

The room was dark. Due to Papa's absence, the shutters hadn't been opened and the lamps hadn't been lit. I couldn't risk turning on the gaslight, so I carried the book over to the window and pushed the heavy wooden shutter open enough to read. I flipped through the pages, looking for the year 1827. That was the year Sean O'Brien stopped getting letters from Maggie. It was so long ago that Papa's careful handwriting had given way to that of his father's.

I had just found the proper year when I heard a change in Katherine's voice.

"Oh, poor Oliver Twist. Poor, poor Oliver Twist," she said.

There was no time to put the book back. I dropped it and ran to the doors, hoping I could slip out before I was seen. But at just that moment, Katherine took a deep breath and nodded.

"Oh good. Someone is helping him. Oliver Twist will be all right," she said.

I took a deep breath and with shaking hands went back to the ledger. I ran my finger down the column of names, their positions, and their wages. I looked for names that had extra notations, and there it was—Maggie O'Brien! I read everything as quickly as I could, committing it to memory, and then put the book back.

I had just closed the doors to Papa's study when the main doors to the library opened again.

Katherine jumped out of her chair and strode toward the sofa.

"Everything all right, ladies?" Mr. Fellows asked. He had a piece of paper in his hands. No doubt the wine inventory I had told him Papa wanted.

Katherine nodded. "I was very worried about Oliver Twist, but he has managed to escape the Beadle."

Mr. Fellows eyed me all away across the room. I was

leaning on the doors to the study, far from Katherine and the book.

"I was too provoked to sit still," I said to him. "Poor Oliver Twist!"

"Perhaps another book would serve you better," Mr. Fellows said dryly.

Katherine snapped the book shut. "I think you're right, Mr. Fellows. In fact, I think Lady Elizabeth and I had rather go for a walk before lunch. We were quite taken over by the story."

"Whatever you say, milady," Mr. Fellows said with a bow. He entered Papa's study and placed the paper on his desk, looking around to make sure all was as it should be. He stopped short, looking at the shutters, and closed the one I had left ajar.

If the butler knew I had been snooping, he said nothing. "I'll let the footman know you'll be needing your parasols," he said, and left the library.

I ran over to Katherine and took her hands. "Maggie O'Brien *did* work here, just when Mr. O'Brien said she did. She disappeared after taking a holiday. No one knows what happened to her. There's a notation in the book about it, and her wages were put aside for her."

"Oh, that is too bad," Katherine said. "We won't be able to tell Mr. O'Brien what happened to her."

"Maybe we can—the book says that she shared a room with another kitchen maid named Clarice."

"We still have a kitchen maid named Clarice," Katherine said, her voice rising.

"We must convince Essie to talk to her and find out what happened."

Katherine shook her head. "We can't ask Essie to do that. She's far too nervous about losing her position. We can't put her at risk like that, Elizabeth."

I knew Katherine was right. That left us with only one option.

"We could talk to Clarice ourselves, without Essie knowing," I said.

"I do hate to keep secrets from Essie," Katherine answered. "And if Papa finds out, he'll be unhappy with us. So will Mr. Fellows."

"But we have to risk it—for Mr. O'Brien. We have to find out what happened to his Maggie."

Katherine bit her lip nervously. I could tell she was trying to come up with another idea, one that carried less of a risk with it.

But we were out of options. Finally, she nodded her head, having reached the same conclusion I had moments before: The only option we had was to somehow talk to Clarice ourselves.

6

On our walk, Katherine and I tried to think of a way we could talk to Clarice alone. It wasn't going to be easy. The servants' hall and the kitchen were always buzzing with activity, and Mr. Fellows clearly desired us to stop going downstairs at all.

"We simply have to keep slipping downstairs until we can find Clarice on her own," I said, "no matter what Mr. Fellows believes about ladies being downstairs."

"He'll know we're up to something if he keeps finding us," Katherine said. "Essie will as well."

"Not with the birthday ball just a week away," I answered. "We'll use that as our excuse!"

Over the next two days, we managed to slip away from Essie twice by making up errands for her to run. We ventured downstairs only to be waylaid by Mrs. Cosgrove or Mrs. Fields with questions. Mrs. Cosgrove wanted us to approve the flower arrangements. Mrs. Fields wanted us to taste a new hors d'oeuvre or the small practice cakes she had made to be certain they were what we expected. The flowers and the cakes were indeed beautiful and delicious, but I felt thwarted and disappointed at every turn.

One afternoon, I thought I saw Clarice alone, stirring a pot of soup. We had just entered the kitchen when Mr. Fellows pounced like a cat on a mouse, telling us to go back upstairs and ring for Essie.

We were turning to leave when we heard a lucky piece of news. Mrs. Fields let Clarice know that she was to launder all of the linens for the birthday ball the next afternoon. "And you'll have to do it alone, I'm afraid. Mildred is down with a cold, and Gertie's taking her half day."

"That's it," I whispered to Katherine as soon as we were upstairs again. "We'll talk to Clarice while she's doing laundry."

Katherine shuddered. "In the basement?" she asked.

We knew the maids avoided the basement whenever they could. Essie said they believed it was haunted. Katherine and I were down there only once, during a game of hide-and-seek on our eighth birth-day. Katherine was sure she saw a ghost, not to mention a mouse or two.

I nodded, willing to brave the damp, dark cellar to discover the truth about Maggie O'Brien. "The base-ment—right after luncheon."

Essie came upon us in the great hall. "Mr. Fellows said you needed something," she said.

"We wanted to admire the cakes again," Katherine said.

"Is that what you were whispering about, then?" Essie asked.

"Only the party," I answered quickly. "And the boys we'll dance with."

"Your first dance, after Lord Chatswood, will be with your cousin Maxwell," Essie reminded me. "After all, he will be your husband someday, and won't it be lovely to say that you danced together at your twelfth birthday ball?"

I made a face, but agreed. Cousin Maxwell was perfectly nice, but why was I constantly reminded that he would one day be my husband?

"I hope a boy asks me to dance," Katherine said

with a laugh. "How terrible to have to dance with an old uncle or something while Elizabeth is dancing a reel with Maxwell."

"I'm sure a nice boy will ask you to dance, Lady Katherine," Essie said. "You and Lady Elizabeth will be the stars of the party."

Katherine did a little twirl. "And we'll be wearing the prettiest dresses."

"Speaking of your lovely dresses, Madame Dubois will be back tomorrow right after luncheon for your final fittings," Essie said.

"Tomorrow?" I asked, my heart sinking. That was exactly the time Clarice would be alone in the basement. "Can't we put her off?"

"It wouldn't do to wait, Lady Elizabeth," Essie said, giving me a curious look. "What if the dresses aren't perfect?"

"No, of course not," I said. "I had just forgotten." It was hard enough to evade Essie, Mr. Fellows, and the rest of the servants. Now we'd have to somehow escape Madame Dubois, too.

I thought about it while Essie led us upstairs to dress for dinner. She and Katherine talked of dresses and dancing and boys. My mind was on other things.

"Don't worry," I whispered to my twin while Essie was distracted for a moment. "I have a plan."

Later that night, after Essie helped us get ready for bed and said good night, Katherine and I met in the dressing closet. Our pile of food had clearly grown. I had straightened it up a number of times, only to find it toppled again. That morning, I had even managed to snag a half-empty jar of Mrs. Fields's delicious plum preserves from the breakfast table.

Katherine came and plopped onto my bed with me. "Now, tell me your plan."

Between Essie, who seemed to know we had a secret, Mr. Fellows, and Papa, I hadn't a minute to tell her about my secret plot to talk to Clarice.

"Madame Dubois can't tell us apart anyway," I said. "You'll have to be both me and you for the dress fitting, and I'll go to the basement to talk to Clarice."

"Alone?" Katherine asked, her eyes wide. "Won't you be frightened?"

I shook my head, ignoring the nervous fluttering of my heart.

"What about Essie?" Katherine asked.

"She hardly ever stays for the fittings," I reminded her. "She said she had to walk to the village tomorrow. I'll make sure she goes right after her own luncheon. Madame Dubois can help us undress."

I heard a scuttling noise and sat up. Could Essie be spying on us?

Katherine heard it too. She kissed my cheek and ran through the dressing closet to her own bed. On the count of three, we said our "sweet dreams" and blew out our candles.

I could hardly wait for the next afternoon when I might finally find out the cause of Maggie O'Brien's mysterious disappearance.

I watched from the drawing room window as Madame Dubois arrived in one of Papa's carriages. Essie would be finishing up her lunch any minute and walking to the village. I was afraid she might find a reason not to run her own errand, so I added one of my own. I had asked her to choose a red ribbon for me at the store on High Street and put it on Papa's account. Katherine had asked for a blue one. We had ribbons enough, certainly, but Essie didn't question our request.

"You hurry upstairs," I whispered to Katherine. "While the footman's back is turned, I'll slip down to the servants' hall. I must make my way to the cellar stairs before they finish their luncheon."

Katherine and I walked together into the great hall. Then, just as the footman began to open the door for Madame, I slipped though the servants' door and Katherine dashed upstairs.

I could hear the servants at their luncheon, talking and laughing, full of excitement about the ball. I had worried the extra work would cause some friction, so I was pleased to hear them sound so happy.

I tiptoed past their dining room toward the door to the cellar. A chair scraped across the floor and I heard Mrs. Fields's distinctive voice.

"That's it, then. Back to work."

I had just a second or two before they all entered the hall, heading to their afternoon duties. Quickly, I opened the cellar door. I cringed when it let out a loud squeak but was on the other side of it before anyone could see me.

I cringed even harder when the door closed behind

me. Gaslight had never been installed here. The basement was spooky and dark. Why didn't I think to bring a candle? I reached the bottom of the stairs and felt the sticky threads of a cobweb break against my face. I brushed them away frantically, hoping their creator hadn't landed in my hair.

Then I heard a tinkling sound—a ghostly bell. I was tempted to turn around and run right back upstairs, but I forced myself to walk down the dark hall to the laundry area. I had promised Sean O'Brien, and I would keep my promise. With my next step, I nearly laughed, realizing that the eerie bell was my own chatelaine.

In the laundry, a small window near the ceiling, partly covered by a hedge, let in a small amount of light. I took a deep breath to steady myself and waited for Clarice.

A few moments later I heard a scuffle coming toward me. Was it a mouse? A light seemed to flicker. I jumped back and nearly screamed when a ghostly presence entered the room. But it was only Clarice, carrying a candle in one hand and a mound of white linens in the other.

The maid was just as startled as I; she dropped the

linens and jumped back with a terrified whimper.

"It's me, Clarice. Lady Elizabeth," I said, stepping out of my corner.

"Milady, oh, I am sorry. I thought . . ." Her voice trailed off and she corrected herself, curtsying quickly. "How can I help, milady? Let me lead you back upstairs. We can—"

"I'm sorry I startled you," I said, cutting her off. "I must speak with you alone, and this is the only place that affords us privacy."

"Speak to *me*, Lady Elizabeth?"

"You and Maggie O'Brien shared a room when she worked here twenty years ago, did you not?"

Clarice nodded, her eyes suddenly wary.

"What can you tell me about her?"

"Oh, milady, Mr. Fellows told us not to speak of her when Essie made inquiries last week. He gave strict orders, and I've no desire to lose my position."

"I won't let that happen to you, Clarice. I just want to give a sad man some information about his long-lost wife. I promise that your good name and position won't be in any danger."

The wariness left her face and she softened a bit.

"You remember Maggie O'Brien, don't you?" I asked.

"Oh, indeed I do, milady. We were two young girls together, starting out in service. Only Maggie had grander dreams—she wanted to be a teacher."

"That's the Maggie Sean O'Brien spoke of," I said, excitement bubbling in my chest.

"She tried to teach me to read," Clarice said with a smile. "I never could. The letters danced about the page so! But I didn't let on to Maggie. She tried so hard and was pleased as punch when I finally seemed to catch on. The truth was that she had just the one book and I had memorized the words. It was a harmless fib, and it made her so happy."

"Do you remember when Maggie left?" I asked.

Clarice shook her head. "I was on my yearly holiday, visiting my family in Wales. When I got back, Maggie had gone without ever saying good-bye. I missed her terribly. She was a sweet girl, and a hard worker."

"Did Maggie ever mention a husband?" I asked.

"Oh no, milady. Married girls weren't taken into service. Maggie wouldn't have been hired if she had a husband."

"So she could have had a husband and kept him a secret," I said, thinking aloud.

"I'm sure I don't know anything about that," Clarice replied. "Though I always *thought* she ran away to be married. That's frowned upon when you're in service."

I remembered that Maggie's family thought she might have gotten tired of waiting for Sean and that she had run away with another man. "Did she have a suitor?" I asked.

"Not that I know of, milady, and she wasn't the type to keep secrets, not like some. Except about her box, that is."

"Her box?" I asked.

"Maggie kept her wages in an old wooden box under a loose floorboard in our room. Letters, too," Clarice explained. "It was the first thing I checked when I learned that Maggie had disappeared. I thought for sure she would've taken it with her, but it was still there under the floor. She hadn't locked it, but that's an easy thing to forget. There were some letters on top, and her wages were there. The key was hidden in a corner of the bureau, like always."

"What happened to the box?" I asked.

"I locked it and gave it to the butler—Mr. Adams he was then—for safekeeping. I held on to the key though. I wanted her wages to be safe in case she ever came back for them."

"Do you know what Mr. Adams did with the box?"

"It must still be here in the basement, in the storeroom just down the hall," Clarice said. "I hid the key in the library, behind a big blue book. I used to see it when I was dusting, and then one day it was gone."

"Can you take me to the box?" I asked.

"This way, milady," she said, taking her candle and leading me down the hall. She was just about to open the door to the storeroom when we heard a loud squeak. Clarice gasped. "The door, milady. Someone's coming. You can't be found here!"

7

Clarice pulled me to the other side of the hall as the footsteps neared. "I'm sorry, milady. You must hurry," she pleaded.

I wondered where she intended to hide me when she pushed against what appeared to be a solid wall. Then a door appeared like magic.

"A secret passage, milady," she said, seeing the question on my face.

An unlit candle sat in a nook just inside the door and Clarice used hers to light it for me. "Follow this hall until you reach the stairs, then take them until you find a door on your right. You'll be in the library."

A secret passage, how exciting! I thought. My excitement waned as the door closed behind me and I was left alone. The darkness seemed to swallow the light of my candle. With careful steps, one hand holding the candle in front of me and the other touching the cold, damp stone of the wall, I moved forward, jumping at every noise. I could practically feel the presence of ancient ghosts. I tried to stop my imagination from running wild, but I couldn't help wondering if any of those ancient ghosts had used this passage for vile deeds.

My candle flickered and I feared it would go out, so I took my hand off the wall and cupped my fingers around it. I was unsettled in the dark and moved as quickly as I could, but I feared I would trip on the rough stone floor. Finally, I banged my toes against the stairs Clarice had spoken of.

I held my candle aloft to judge their height. They were steep and curved and I couldn't see the top. What if they didn't lead to the library? What if they went up and up and up and I found myself in a gloomy attic cell never to be found? What if Maggie O'Brien had walked these very stairs thinking they were a shortcut, only to disappear? I shivered at the idea of stumbling onto her skeleton, her final words etched into the wall with the tip of her fingernail.

Stop this silliness! I told myself. *Clarice wouldn't send*

you into danger. I squared my shoulders and mustered my courage. The library was two full stories above the cellar. Of course I wouldn't be able to see the top of a curving staircase by the light of one lone candle. The draft that had caused my flame to flicker in the hall seemed to be absent on the stair. I held the candle in my left hand and ran my right along the wall, climbing one step at a time.

Finally, I touched something that felt like wood on my right, just where Clarice said the door would be. I listened carefully for a moment in case someone was in the library. Hearing nothing, I gave the door a gentle push. It didn't budge. My heart hammered like the dressing gong at the thought of having to make the reverse trip to the basement. I pushed harder and harder, and the heavy door finally began to move.

Only then did I realize that the door was one of Papa's bookcases. How ingenious!

I had blown out my candle and taken a careful step into the library when I heard Papa's voice. Had I been discovered? But then Papa's clear baritone was met by Mr. Fellows's steady bass rumble. They were in Papa's study. I only hoped they would remain occupied long enough for me to escape the library.

My next task was to get upstairs to my bedchamber without being seen. I poked my head into the great hall—it was empty, thank goodness—and ran up the staircase as quick as a cat. I thought I was out of danger, but I was met by the exclamations of Madame Dubois.

"It is too long," she cried. "The entire hem needs to be redone! How could such a thing have happened? My measurements were precise."

Oh no. Katherine and I had forgotten that I am a half inch taller than she. I had to get in there somehow and fix this, or Essie—and Mr. Fellows—might discover that Katherine was pretending to be me while I was disobeying Papa's orders.

I slipped into Katherine's room and then into the dressing closet. Katherine was waiting for my knock. I only hoped she could hear it above Madame Dubois's exclamations.

"Excuse me, Madame. I must see if Essie has returned from the village," I heard Katherine say.

"*Now*, Lady Elizabeth?" Madame cried. "We have much work to do."

"I'll be just a moment," she said.

I heard the door to my bedchamber close, and seconds later Katherine joined me in her room. "Hurry," she whispered, "or Madame will discover us. How could we forget about the difference in our heights? She's beside herself."

She frantically undid the buttons running up the back of my day dress. I stepped out of it quickly and then tried to do the same with her ball gown. "I don't know how Essie does this so easily," I muttered. There were at least fifty pearl buttons running up the back of the dress.

We heard my bedroom door open and Madame talking to someone in the hall. One of the maids, I guessed. "Do find Lady Elizabeth for me at once and beg her to return. We must avert this disaster."

I heard the maid mumble her reply and then the sound of footsteps as she rushed off to find me.

Katherine was finally able to step out of the ball gown and I stepped into it. Her fingers, as clumsy as mine with the tiny buttons, raced to fasten everything as it had been. Finally, overheated and out of breath, I ran through the dressing closet and into my own room.

In a moment I was standing on the low stool in front of Madame. She had scissors in hand, ready to undo my hem.

"Milady, we don't have time—" She stopped short and took a slow walk around the stool, stopping to fasten a couple of buttons that Katherine had missed. Then she pulled on my skirt. It reached just to the bottom of my slippers, as it should. "What has happened?" she asked, eyeing me suspiciously. "It is perfect."

"It was the shoes, Madame. I had on the wrong shoes," I answered with a sweet smile. "They were in Lady Katherine's bedchamber. It was a foolish mistake, and I am sorry to have caused you distress."

Madame lifted my skirt with the edge of her scissors and looked at my shoes, dusty from the basement. She was about to say something about the state of them when she let out the loudest screech I had ever heard. Before I knew what was happening, the dressmaker had leaped to the top of the stool with me and clutched my shoulders in an iron grip.

Lady Katherine, her day dress half unfastened, ran into my room from her own, preceded by a gray streak.

She, too, screamed and leaped onto the stool with Madame and me.

"What is it?" she screamed. "What is wrong?"

Just then, I spotted a family of frightened mice run under my bed, followed by another ear-piercing scream from Madame Dubois. I believe she would have climbed onto my shoulders if she could, to put a greater distance between the mice and herself.

Mr. Fellows, Papa, Papa's valet, Essie, a footman, Mrs. Cosgrove, and two housemaids all burst into my room.

Madame was taking deep, gulping breaths, trying to calm herself.

"What is it?" Papa yelled. "What has happened?"

Madame Dubois, her face white, gingerly stepped down from the stool, standing on her tiptoes. "Please forgive me for taking such a liberty, milady," she said to me. Then she turned to Papa. "A rat, sir. Many rats, in fact. An entire army of rats."

Mrs. Cosgrove gasped. Mr. Fellows stared at the poor housekeeper with such a look of righteous indignation you might think she had committed murder.

It was taking every bit of her courage for the

dressmaker not to run from the room. In fact, if a group of servants weren't blocking the door, I think she would have.

I could feel my lips twitching, and I pressed them together so as not to laugh. "Not rats, Papa. Mice. And just a few. They ran under the bed."

Mrs. Cosgrove met Mr. Fellows's indignation with a heaping platter of her own. "Mice! Upstairs at Chatswood Manor? Well, I never!" She grabbed my fireplace poker and marched over to my bed. Lifting the bedclothes, she poked under the bed, and two mice scampered out, heading back to the dressing closet.

Madame Dubois screamed again and jumped up onto a chair. Papa helped her to sit down, sending one of the maids for a glass of wine to steady her. If it weren't too undignified, I think the dressmaker would have raised her feet up into the air.

Mrs. Cosgrove was giving Essie and one of the housemaids a stern eye. "We will be discussing this later, and no mistake," she announced. "There has been a serious breach in cleaning if mice are allowed to run wild in the family rooms."

It was as if a mouse had heard her, because at that

moment one of them made a run for it, rushing toward my bedroom door.

Madame Dubois knocked over her chair trying to get away, and ended up on the floor, exactly where one did not want to be when mice were running about. Her feet were in the air and her hoopskirt sprang up, revealing her petticoats. Mr. Fellows's face turned a shade of bright red I had never seen before, while Mrs. Cosgrove and Papa helped the woman to her feet.

I could feel Katherine's shoulders begin to shake beside me. I had been trying my hardest not to laugh, but now I looked at my sister and I couldn't help but giggle. That set her off too, and soon we were laughing so hard that our stomachs hurt and tears ran down our faces.

A few moments later, when Madame Dubois was once again upright, Mr. Fellows marched into the dressing closet.

"I have discovered the source of the problem, my lord," he said.

Mr. Fellows walked out of the dressing closet carrying a small pile of tea sandwiches.

I could see now, in the bright light of day, that they were covered in small, mouse-sized bites.

"What is the meaning of this?" Papa asked us.

Katherine and I quickly turned serious.

I knew better than to bring up Sean O'Brien's name, but I had to tell Papa the truth about the food. "We're saving food for the people of Ireland," I said.

"We're going to send it to a hungry family there," Katherine added.

"Tea sandwiches?" Mrs. Cosgrove asked weakly. "To Ireland?"

"And just how were you planning to deliver this food to a hungry family?" Papa asked.

"By post," I admitted.

Papa shook his head. "I commend you on your desire to help those less fortunate," he told us. "But sending tea sandwiches by post will not solve the problem. They will be inedible long before they reach Ireland."

I could see now the folly of our plan. My cheeks burned as everyone had a good chuckle at Katherine's and my expense, even Madame Dubois.

"Can't we do *something*, Papa?" I asked.

He shook his head again, even more firmly this time. "I told you the government has the matter well in hand."

The staff began to disperse. Mr. Fellows sent two footmen in search of mousetraps while the house-keeper began to supervise a cleanup.

"Not to worry, Lord Chatswood. We'll have this problem taken care of in no time," Mrs. Cosgrove assured him.

Papa turned to my sister and me. "You've created a lot of extra work for the staff—on top of everything they have to do for your birthday ball. I expect you to make the proper apologies."

"We're sorry, Mrs. Cosgrove," I said.

"Very sorry, Mr. Fellows," Katherine added.

Mrs. Cosgrove sighed. "You've got good hearts, and you meant no harm."

"Our apologies for frightening you, Madame," I said.

The dressmaker waved her hand weakly. Her eyes flitted about, still looking for mice. "The fittings are done. I will leave the dresses with you. Perhaps your maid can take over."

"Yes, ma'am," Essie said to Madame. "I'll handle things from here."

Mr. Fellows gave the poor woman his arm, and with mincing steps, she tiptoed out of the room.

"Come, Lady Elizabeth," Essie said. "We'll get you back into your day dress." She looked around for it, expecting to find it waiting for me on my bed. Instead, it was in Katherine's room.

"I'll get it," I said, jumping off the stool.

Essie might have followed me and discovered the dress in a heap on the floor—something Madame would never do—but she was distracted by Lady Katherine. Only a few of her buttons were fastened, and those that were, were cockeyed.

"Are you ladies up to something?" Essie asked. "Something besides hiding food? There are some strange goings-on here."

"No, Essie," I said innocently, holding my dress out to her. "We're just excited about the party."

As soon as Katherine and I were alone, I pulled her outside for a walk on the grounds so that I could tell her about Clarice without being overheard.

"Do you think the box will solve the puzzle of what happened to Maggie?" Katherine asked.

"I think it must. Clarice said there were letters on top," I answered. "We just have to go back to the cellar to find the box."

But getting back to the cellar proved to be more difficult than I could have imagined. Our every moment was spoken for with preparations for the ball, not to mention the fact that the staff was constantly bustling about.

Twice Katherine and I tried to sneak down to the cellar—once through the servants' area and once through the secret passage in the library—but both times we were thwarted by Essie. Our lady's maid was growing more suspicious by the moment, but every time she tried to discover the source of our strange behavior, we claimed birthday excitement.

I did hate lying to her, but I hated the idea of disappointing Sean O'Brien even more.

Mr. O'Brien was due to return the day after our birthday. Finally, the night before our ball, we realized that we'd have to sneak down to the cellar as soon as the house settled for the night. The ghostly cellar was the last place I wanted to be at night, but I felt I had no choice.

That night, Katherine and I fought to stay awake. We heard Papa come upstairs a couple of hours after Essie had wished us good night. Shortly thereafter, we heard his valet make his way downstairs. We tiptoed into the hall and heard the quiet rumble of Mr. Fellows instructing the footmen to ensure that all the lamps were extinguished.

A few moments later, it was time to try our luck. "Let's go," I whispered.

I was about to step onto the stairs when Katherine's hand on my arm held me back. She was just in time.

Mr. Fellows began to make his way up the staircase, candle in hand!

Quickly, we slipped back into my bedchamber. I looked at Katherine, her wide, frightened eyes a mirror of my own as Mr. Fellows stopped in front of my door. He did not enter though, and a moment later we heard his footsteps make their way down the hall.

"He's checking to make sure everything is settled for the night," Katherine whispered in my ear, her lips hardly moving.

We waited as the butler patrolled the hall, ensuring our safety and comfort. Finally, after what seemed like hours, we heard his tread on the stairs again just as the clock was chiming midnight.

More carefully this time, I waited for the clock to chime the quarter hour, at which point I decided it was safe to venture out. I had never seen the house so dark. A lone lamp burned in the hall and another at the bottom of the stairs in the great hall. Katherine and I held hands and tiptoed, too frightened to even utter a word, and slipped into the library.

Once inside, I wondered how to find the secret door in the dark, but I moved from bookshelf to bookshelf, tugging on each, until I found the correct one. Finally, at the top of the stairs, I deemed it safe to light the candle I had left behind two days ago with the matches on the shelf. There was another candle on the ledge, which I lit for Katherine.

I held my candle aloft, and together Katherine and I looked down the staircase. The steepness of it made me dizzy for a moment. My sister shivered, and not from the cold, although the air held a damp chill. It was a long way down, and no one knew where we were. If we were hurt or got lost, it could be days before we were found.

"One step at a time," I whispered to Katherine.

We made our slow way down. As we rounded one of the curves, a draft whooshed past us like a ghost, blowing out my candle. Every part of me wanted to turn around and run back upstairs, but I forced myself to stay put.

Thank goodness Katherine had been cupping her flame at that very moment. With shaking hands, she relit my candle and on we went. Finally, we reached the rough wooden door that would lead us into the cellar.

The cellar itself was even spookier in the night

than it was in the daytime. I quickly led Katherine to the storage room and described the plain wooden box Clarice had told me about. Katherine checked the shelves on one side of the room, while I checked the other.

I found it, covered in dust and spiderwebs. "It's here!" I yelled, and then quickly clapped my hand over my mouth. My voice seemed to echo about the room and perhaps the entire cellar. We stood frozen on the spot, listening for a cry of discovery, but none came. The servants were either all asleep or far enough away not to hear. I only hoped that the old ghosts decided we were beneath their notice.

Katherine's face was pale and strained as she joined me. I gave the box a shake. There was definitely paper inside. Maggie O'Brien's wages and her letters.

Quickly, quietly, I led Katherine back to the secret staircase. The climb seemed shorter now that we had made our discovery, and although our candles flick-ered, the ancient ghosts were kind enough not to blow them out. Perhaps they, too, wanted Sean O'Brien to find his Maggie.

Leaving our candles where we had found them,

we slipped back into the library. In moments we were racing up the grand staircase and slipping back into my room. The single candles Essie had left for us still flickered on our nightstands.

"Shall we open it?" Katherine asked, breathless.

"It's locked," I told her. "Besides, Mr. O'Brien should be the one to discover its secrets."

She nodded. "The day after tomorrow," she whispered. "I can hardly wait."

"But first—our birthday," I told her. "And our birthday ball!"

9

The next morning, I was awakened when Essie drew open my curtains, letting the sun shine in.

"Happy birthday to you, milady," she sang, walking through the dressing closet to Katherine's room. "Happy birthday, Lady Katherine," she said.

I groaned and rolled over, burrowing under my comforter to block the light. It felt as if I had just fallen asleep. "What's the time?" I asked.

"It's nearly half past ten, Lady Elizabeth," Essie said. "His Lordship has been waiting for you to join him at breakfast for ever so long. Cook has something special prepared."

Essie came back into my room and pulled the covers from over my head. "Come, ladies. It's not like you to sleep this late. What were you two up to last night?"

I sat up then. Katherine came into my room behind Essie, her eyes wide.

"We were up late talking about our birthday," I said, rubbing my eyes.

I could tell she didn't believe me, especially when she turned to my twin with the same question.

Katherine shrugged and wrinkled her nose. "I suppose we were too filled with excitement to fall asleep and then too tired to wake up again," she said.

Essie shook her head. "I hope you're not too tired to enjoy your party," she said. "Now, hurry. We mustn't keep His Lordship waiting any longer that we already have."

Papa waited for us in the dining room, and the entire household staff came in to wish us a happy birthday. Then Cook proudly had the footmen bring in platters of all of our favorite breakfast foods—coddled eggs, sausages, and hot toast with sweet butter and marmalade. There was a pyramid of fruit on the table and two mini birthday cakes, one each for Katherine and me.

"A preview of tonight's cakes," Mrs. Fields said.

"I thought you might enjoy a small taste after your breakfast."

"Thank you, Mrs. Fields. They look delicious."

"You've outdone yourself," Katherine added, clapping her hands.

The staff filed out, and Papa teased us about sleeping the day away while we ate our feast.

When we finished, Papa turned to Mr. Fellows. "I think we're ready for the tray, Fellows."

Katherine and I exchanged a glance. It was time for birthday presents!

Mr. Fellows brought in a silver tray with velvet boxes on top, one tied with a red ribbon and one with blue. There were also two letters written on Mama's creamy white stationery. My heart gave a little flip when I recognized my name written in her hand on one of them.

Mr. Fellows handed the tray to Papa and then left the room, closing the door behind him.

"I want to take this occasion to tell both of you just how proud I am of the young ladies you've become," Papa said. "Your mama—"

Papa's voice caught, and he had to clear his throat.

My own eyes filled, and when I dared a glance at my twin, I saw that Katherine too was blinking away tears.

"Your mama was also very proud of you," he said. "We talked about that just a few weeks before she left us. It was her dearest wish that you would always love and support each other. And I've seen in these difficult weeks that her wish has come true."

Katherine and I smiled at each other through our tears. Without my sister's support, I would not have survived losing Mama. And I knew Katherine felt the same about me.

"Your mother always said you were your best selves when you remembered your love for each other, and she chose a special gift for each of you to remind you always of your bond."

Papa handed us each a velvet box—mine was the one tied with the red ribbon, of course.

Inside was a stunning gold pendant. It was shaped like half a heart and set with rubies that glittered in the sunlight streaming through the window. I pressed it against my heart, realizing that the last hand to hold it had been Mama's.

"Oh, Papa," I breathed. "I'll cherish it forever."

It was only then that I looked across the table to see that Katherine held the other half of the heart, only hers was studded with sapphires as blue as the summer sky.

"Now I must show you what makes these necklaces even more special," Papa said. He held out his hands, and we each placed our pendant in them. Then Papa slid the two halves of the heart together to form a single, perfect heart.

I started to say something, but Papa held a finger to his lips and motioned us to lean in and listen.

Click. Click, whirrrrrrr.

I heard the sound of a clockwork mechanism, like that of a music box, and then the quiet creaking of a hinge. Papa turned the necklace over to reveal that a secret panel had opened on the back of the heart when the two halves were joined together.

A secret compartment! The excitement in Katherine's face reflected what I was feeling. I loved the necklace even more because I knew that Mama had chosen it for us—two halves of a whole.

Papa slid the necklaces apart and fastened them

around our necks. The minute it touched my skin, falling just over my own heart, I knew I would wear this necklace until I passed it down to my own daughter.

As much as I loved the necklace, I knew that the tray held letters written by Mama. These would be her last words to me, and I took my envelope with trembling fingers. Like me, Papa was too overcome with emotion to speak.

I read my letter silently, wiping away bittersweet tears. My heart swelled with Mama's love and advice, and I vowed to make her proud of me. I would be the daughter and sister she wished me to be.

When we had all had a good cry and gotten ahold of ourselves again, I offered to read my letter to Katherine and Papa.

9 January 1848

My dearest daughter,

The fates have not been kind to us that my life should dim at the dawn of your adulthood. It is my greatest regret that I will

not live to see you and your sister as women
grown, married, perhaps mothers to girls of
your own. I hold hope that the hole I leave
in your life will be filled many times over with
others who will cherish you as much as I
do. Yet there may come times when you wish
you could seek my counsel, and so I write
this letter now for whenever you find yourself
longing for your mother's advice.

I had to take a deep breath in order to continue.
There were so many times already that I longed for
Mama's advice.

My sweet child, it has been my privilege
to watch you grow for the past eleven—
nearly twelve—years. And though your
childhood has yet to end, your father and
I have been charged with the challenging
task of deciding your future. Let me assure
you that our decision was made with great

care. When you are of age, you will marry your cousin Maxwell Tynne to fulfill the rules of inheritance. Maxwell is an honest and honorable young man and, I think, well suited for you. It is my great hope that your marriage will be a long and happy one, filled with love.

I wonder if you have noticed yet how others look to you to lead them. Doubtless they are drawn to your strength, which I see reflected even in the fiery hues of your favorite color; your dedication to your family; your commitment to everyone you meet; and your compassion for those less fortunate. Daughter, you have been graced with all the characteristics you will need as the next lady of Chatswood Manor.

The hour grows late, and I still have one more letter to write before I retire. And so,

my darling Elizabeth, I will conclude here.
Please know today, tomorrow, and every day
of your life how very proud you've made me
and how very much I love you.

    Your loving mother

    I had to take a moment to compose myself before I could look up from my letter. I folded it and pressed it to my heart. Finally, when I was able to speak, I saw that Papa's and Katherine's cheeks were wet also with tears.

    Katherine wiped her eyes and began to read her own letter. It began much the same as mine, filled with Mama's regret about not being able to see us grow up and marry and have children of our own. When it came the subject of our future lives, however, the letters differed.

    Your grace, elegance, and the air of
peace you carry with you always, reflected
in the soothing tones of your favorite color,

inspire everyone around you to be their best.
You have the soul of a poet and an artist.
When you are of age, I hope you will seize
every bright, new prospect that comes your
way. You have all the characteristics you
need to live life to its fullest and embrace the
new opportunities available to the adventurous
women of our times.

When the time is right, I hope you meet
a wonderful man and marry for love. I wish
you a long, happy marriage filled with love
and children. Daughter, you have everything
you need to lead a rich, fulfilling life.

I know you will always value your family
above all else and that you and your dear
sister will love and support each other forever.

I must conclude now, my darling
Katherine. Please know today, tomorrow, and

*every day of your life how very proud you've
made me and how very much I love you.*

Your loving mother

Katherine and I embraced each other, vowing to love each other forever, just as Mama wished.

"I am very proud of both of you," Papa said, blinking away tears. "And I know your mama is, too."

At that moment, Mr. Fellows discreetly opened the door. "Milord, we really must let the staff into the room to prepare for the ball," he said.

"Yes, of course, Fellows," Papa said, ushering us toward the door. "It's time for you two to start thinking about whatever young ladies think about when they're getting ready for a ball."

Katherine and I smiled, shaking off our sadness.

"The ball!" I said. Then I thought about our dresses. "Our necklaces are going to look perfect with our ball gowns!"

Katherine and I went upstairs to put Mama's letters in a special place. I knew I would read mine many, many times.

We found Essie checking the mousetraps in Katherine's room. "Nothing caught for two days now, Lady Katherine," she announced. "I think we've completely eradicated Madame Dubois's 'army of rats.'"

I couldn't help but giggle, remembering how terrified the dressmaker had been and her hopeless efforts to appear dignified at the same time.

Essie turned toward me and gasped when she saw our necklaces. "Oh, how beautiful," she said. "I knew Lady Mary had something very special planned for this birthday, but I never imagined anything so perfect."

"They *are* perfect," I said.

"Mama wanted them to remind us that we must always love and support each other," Katherine said.

She held up her half of the heart. "I will always love my sister, Elizabeth," she said.

"And I will always love my sister, Katherine," I answered, doing the same.

The second the two halves came together, we heard the miniature gears turning, and the secret panel opened.

"Just like the secret—"

I cut myself off. I couldn't tell Essie about the secret staircase without telling her why we had used it.

Essie turned to me with what was becoming a too-familiar expression—suspicion.

Katherine saw my alarm and jumped in to save me. "Papa told us a secret," she said. "He's very proud of us and said Mama would be proud, too."

Essie smiled, and her eyes softened. "That's no secret, at least not to anyone who's met the two of you. I'm proud of you, too, and no mistake. You're becoming very fine young ladies. And I know you'll cherish those necklaces forever because your dear mother chose them for you," she said.

"I wish you had something of your mother's to remember her by," I said.

"Something to love and cherish," Katherine added. "Like we love you."

"I have the love of two of the finest young ladies in England," Essie said, reaching to pull us close for a hug. "What more could I need?"

Later that morning, with all of the servants busy with party preparations, Katherine and I did our best to stay out of the way. Luncheon was served on a tray in our room. The hours ticked by slowly until Katherine pulled out Mama's trinket box.

"There must be something in here that would look pretty on a bit of ribbon. A necklace we can give to Essie to remind her of how much we care about her," she said.

"That's a wonderful idea," I answered.

We sorted through the trinkets, searching for the perfect thing. And then Katherine found it—a Celtic knot, a symbol of Ireland. There was a long arrow dangling below it, which would point to Essie's heart. We rubbed it with a cloth until it was shiny, and then I found a blue ribbon and Katherine a red one. We twisted them together before attaching them to the knot. The ribbon would remind her of how much we loved her while the knot would be a symbol of her Irish mama.

Finally, after what seemed like three days instead of one afternoon, Essie came to let us know it was time to dress for the ball.

"How does everything look?" I asked.

"Beautiful, milady. You'll be very pleased," she said. "I believe this is the finest Chatswood Manor has ever looked."

"And you're the finest lady's maid," Katherine said, smiling. She handed Essie the necklace we had made for her.

Listening to Essie's exclamations over its beauty, you would have thought the necklace was covered in gemstones, and I told her so.

"But it's covered in something much better, milady. The love of you two girls is worth more to me than all the jewels in the world."

The three of us turned misty once again.

"None of that now, ladies," Essie said, wiping her

own eyes. "I won't send you to your birthday ball with red eyes. Now, who wants her hair done first?"

I sat at my dressing table and watched in the mirror while Essie pulled my hair up into a sophisticated, grown-up knot and tucked small seed-pearl pins around it, alternating with red rosettes to match the red in my dress. Katherine and I had decided to wear our hair exactly the same, only hers would have tiny blue larkspurs instead of red roses.

I stepped into my dress so as not to muss my hair and watched myself in the mirror as Essie fastened the back. The dress's neckline showed off my necklace beautifully. Wearing it, I felt like Mama was nearby, watching over me.

When I was finished and Essie had slipped on my dancing slippers, it was Katherine's turn. I twirled, once, twice, three times around her bedchamber, practicing my waltz while she had her hair done. My dress swirled around me, and I didn't step on my train once. Soon, Katherine joined me, holding my hands as we swept around her bedchamber and Essie clapped. Katherine's sapphires glittered, and I knew my rubies must have been doing the same.

A few moments later, Papa knocked on Katherine's door. Essie opened it to him and then slipped out of the room to join the other servants.

"The guests are gathered in the ballroom," Papa said, "ready to greet the birthday girls." He stopped to admire our dresses. "Are you turning twelve or sixteen?" he asked with a smile. "You'll be leaving me any moment to begin your married lives."

"Papa!" I said. "Don't rush us away. Besides, I will be the lady of Chatswood Manor one day—unless you'd rather I run away and marry a pirate."

"A pirate! Never, my dear girl," he answered. "Cousin Maxwell will do quite well." He kissed my forehead and then Katherine's.

"I'll marry a pirate, then," Katherine teased.

"You will not!" Papa said.

"You look very elegant, Papa," Katherine said, changing the subject.

"Not nearly as elegant as my lovely young ladies," he answered. "I think many young men will be losing their hearts tonight."

Katherine giggled and took one of Papa's arms. I took the other. We walked to the grand staircase leading to the great hall, and I gasped at the beauty of it. All the chandeliers were ablaze, and flowers graced every table. There were vases of red roses, blue larkspur, and white lilies.

The staff waited for us in two lines at the bottom of the staircase. Mr. Fellows and Mrs. Cosgrove were at the front of the line, as always. Next to Mrs. Cosgrove was Mrs. Fields. I looked for Clarice but soon realized that she and the rest of the kitchen maids must be in the kitchen, busy with the food.

Papa's valet and Essie also stood in positions of prominence, followed by the footmen, the housemaids, and other members of the vast staff.

They all looked up at Katherine and me, and I felt my heart swell with too many emotions—pride, happiness, nervous excitement, and the longing for Mama that always lurked underneath the rest.

As the three of us took our first step onto the staircase, the staff began to applaud. All of those feelings in my heart were now overwhelmed by one emotion: love. I saw it in Katherine's face too, and Papa's. We had the best staff in the world at Chatswood Manor.

As soon as we reached the bottom of the stairs,

Mr. Fellows stepped forward to wish us a happy birthday on behalf of the entire staff.

"Many happy returns of the day, Lady Elizabeth. Lady Katherine," he said.

I leaned forward and kissed the man on the cheek, as did Katherine. Our very formal butler was flustered by our unusual display of affection, but he quickly regained his dignity.

A moment later, the staff was back in full party mode, rushing about to take care of everything that needed to be done for the comfort of our guests.

Mr. Fellows threw open the doors of the ballroom. "Lord Chatswood, Earl of Chatswood Manor," he announced. "Accompanied by Lady Elizabeth Chatswood and Lady Katherine Chatswood."

The guests pressed forward to get a good look at us, and once again there was clapping. There was such a crush of people that it was hard to see who was there, but Papa led us on a promenade around the ballroom to greet our guests. As in the great hall, the chandeliers were ablaze. Ladies' jewels sparkled, and I reached up to touch my ruby-studded heart and felt as if Mama was looking down at me.

The flowers in the ballroom were the purple ones we had requested, combining my favorite color, red, with Katherine's blue. They adorned the walls, were woven through the chandeliers, and enormous vases of every type of purple flower were placed on either side of the orchestra. I knew they would grace the tables in the dining room as well.

I waved to Cousin Cecily, who looked regal in a dress of green silk organza with a green-and-gold brocade bodice. Her mother, my aunt Margaret, stepped forward to tell Katherine and me that we were the picture of Mama, while Cecily held my necklace in her hand for a moment to admire its beauty.

Katherine was nearer to Maxwell Tynne and his family than I was, and they exchanged a word, while I greeted the Clarksons and the Smythes.

Once we had made a complete circle of the room, Papa nodded to the orchestra, and they began to play a waltz. As I was the eldest, he swept me into his arms, and together we spun around the dance floor. Our guests' faces blurred as he twirled me around to the music. I almost giggled when I heard my dancing master's voice in my head, reminding me to hold my arms steady and to stay on my toes.

Too soon, Papa twirled me back to where Katherine stood, and it was her chance to dance with him. Her eyes sparkled and her cheeks were pink with happiness. My sister never had to be reminded to stay on her toes and keep her arms firm. She had a natural elegance that I lacked.

When the waltz was over, Papa brought my sister back to me. The orchestra struck up a reel, and our guests began to take to the dance floor. I had a brief moment of panic. What if no one asked me to dance? By the way Katherine squeezed my hand, I could tell she had the same fear. We both breathed a sigh of relief when we spotted Cousin Maxwell making his way toward us. Behind him, looking sheepish and shy, were Charles Clarkson and Edward Smythe.

Cousin Maxwell bowed to my sister while the other two boys hung back, out of earshot.

"May I have this dance, Lady Elizabeth?" Maxwell asked.

Katherine's cheeks went from pink to red and then were nearly the same purple as our flowers, but her eyes danced with excitement. "I'm Lady Katherine," she said.

Now it was Maxwell's turn to blush, but clearly there was something about my sister that drew his attention more than I did. I laughed, as much to spare their feelings as to save myself. I would much rather dance with Charles or Edward before I had to take the dance floor with a long string of relatives, including my cousin Maxwell.

"Do dance together, please," I said. "Cousin Maxwell and I can dance later. We have all evening."

"Are you sure?" Katherine asked. She knew, even more than I did, that decorum called for Maxwell to dance the first dance with me, not my twin.

"I'm sure," I said, casting my eyes in the direction of the other boys. "I have other dance partners waiting."

That was all the encouragement they needed. The pair joined the couples on the dance floor, and Edward Smythe stepped forward to offer me his hand, which I happily took.

My partner was rather too shy to offer much conversation, so I was free to keep an eye on Katherine and Maxwell. Their conversation was vigorous and lively, and I had never seen my sister look so beautiful.

Then I noticed that Aunt Edwina kept trying

to signal the couple from the side of the ballroom. They were too intent on each other to notice, and finally my aunt drew her husband into the dance. I knew that a lady should never lead on the dance floor, but nevertheless, I led my partner in the same direction and reached the couple just when my aunt and uncle did.

"Maxwell," his mother said, "you are dancing with the wrong sister. You were to dance the first dance with Lady Elizabeth."

Maxwell's face fell and Katherine looked away with a guilty expression, but I only laughed. "Surely *you* can tell us apart, Aunt Edwina. I'm not Elizabeth. I'm Katherine," I said.

My aunt glanced at my necklace and at the red accents on my gown.

"Elizabeth and I have confused a good many people, but I never imagined you would be one of them," I teased.

Aunt Edwina laughed and she looked at Katherine again, shaking her head. "I see it now. I'm am sorry, Elizabeth," she said to my sister. "Dance on, Maxwell."

After many dances, Maxwell accompanied Katherine and me into the dining room. The tables were covered with delicious-looking food. The flowers were in full bloom, and festive confetti decorated the tables. The three of us were having a good laugh about the trick we had played on Maxwell's mother when Cousin Cecily came up behind us. I thought perhaps she had overheard our ruse, but she was more focused on our necklaces.

"Your color suits you well," she said to me. "It's daring and strong, while Lady Katherine's blue is more stately and serene."

Katherine and Maxwell barely heard her, so taken were they with talk of the gardens at Chatswood and the new breed of roses the head gardener was cultivating in the greenhouse.

I had danced with my cousin and future husband a few times over the course of the evening, in between waltzes and reels with old uncles, Papa's friends, and some of our neighbors. But Maxwell and I simply didn't have the connection that he and Katherine did. Our conversation was stiff.

It must be because he'll be my husband one day, I

told myself. *It makes us both shy.*

But in my heart, I was a little sad that I didn't enjoy the company of my future husband nearly as much as my sister did.

$\mathcal{T}$he birthday ball was a great triumph. Both Katherine and I were the stars of the evening. Aside from those few moments in the dining room, we barely had a moment to chat. And we both had to do our best to stay out of Aunt Edwina's way lest she discover our trick.

We almost gave ourselves away at the presentation of the cakes, but I made sure that my sister and I stood side by side and held hands while we blew out our candles. There was such a crush of people wishing us happy returns of the day that my aunt couldn't get near to see whose name was on each cake.

As much as I hated to see it end, the party did draw to a close. The Tynnes were the last guests to leave, and I couldn't help but notice that Cousin Maxwell's eyes lingered on my sister for an extra moment. I also noticed that Katherine enjoyed the attention.

Finally, we kissed Papa good night and headed upstairs, where Essie waited to help us into our night-gowns. We told her all about the party, about the dancing especially, and about how delicious the cakes were.

"It was the most wonderful night of my life," Katherine said breathlessly.

Once again, I noticed that Katherine's cheeks were pink, and I suspected Cousin Maxwell had something to do with the wonder of the evening.

"How about you, Lady Elizabeth?" Essie asked.

"Oh yes, it was splendid," I told her, flopping onto my bed. "Absolutely splendid."

"I imagine you'll be ready for a quiet few days after all the excitement," she said.

"But tomorrow will be a big day, too," I said, remembering that Sean O'Brien would be coming back to Chatswood Manor.

"Big how?" Essie asked.

In my tired excitement, I had completely forgotten that Mr. O'Brien's visit was a secret. Katherine stood behind Essie, shaking her head, her eyes warning me to speak no more.

"Only that we have to thank Mrs. Fields and all the staff for giving us such a perfect birthday," I stammered.

Essie seemed alert to the fact that we had a secret, but it was late and we were tired. She didn't press to discover what we were hiding.

After Essie left my bedchamber, Katherine climbed into bed with me, and we had a good laugh about fooling Aunt Edwina.

"We never would have gotten away with such a trick if Mama were alive," I said.

Katherine nodded. "She was the only person in the world who could tell us apart in an instant."

"I missed her tonight," I whispered. "Let's make a pact to honor Mama's words, to always love and support each other," I said.

"And to remember how much we love her—and Papa," Katherine agreed.

Our necklaces were on my nightstand. I took my half of the heart in my hand. "I am Elizabeth, and I love my sister, Katherine," I said.

Katherine raised hers. "I am Katherine, and I love my sister, Elizabeth."

Katherine and I slid the two halves of the heart

together to form a single, perfect heart. "Forever," we said at the same time.

Click. Click, whirrrrrrr.

We heard the gears spinning and the now familiar sound of the hinge opening to reveal the hidden panel.

"We should hide a secret message inside," I whispered.

"Yes," Katherine said. "What should it say? I'm too tired to think."

"Let's decide tomorrow," I said. Then my tired brain did have one thought. "Confetti," I murmured, thinking about the confetti that decorated the table for the party. "We'll write it down and turn it into confetti. Only we'll know what the message says."

The next morning, Katherine and I slept in again, waking only when Essie came and opened the shutters to let the sunshine in. She surprised us with breakfast in bed, and Katherine joined me to eat our feast.

Essie puttered about the room cleaning up while we told her all about the ball, repeating details from last night and adding new ones as we remembered them.

"Did the staff get to have any fun at all?" I asked.

"Oh, we had a grand time," Essie said. "We had a feast of our own, and birthday cake, too. And everyone offered their best wishes for your happy day."

Essie opened my armoire so that I could choose a dress for the day and spotted Maggie's box. "What's this old thing?" she asked.

"Oh, nothing," I said, jumping out of bed to take it. "Just an old box of Mama's."

"I've never seen it before," Essie said.

"I just found it—in the library."

"That dusty thing was in the library?" Essie said. "I'll have to let Mrs. Cosgrove know that the house-maids have been neglecting their work."

"No, Essie," Katherine pleaded. "It was pushed way to the back of a shelf that has the most boring books in the world on it. They wouldn't have known."

Essie was quiet while she helped us dress and then plaited our hair. "And what will you ladies do with yourselves now that the birthday excitement is over?"

"I want to finish my painting of the gardens," I said. I eyed Katherine. Sean O'Brien was coming after luncheon, when the servants would be busy with their own meal. "And a long walk after lunch, I think."

Katherine nodded. "A *very* long walk," she said.

After luncheon, with all the servants safely at their own meal and Papa immersed in the newspaper in the library, Katherine and I ran upstairs for Maggie O'Brien's box. We set out to meet her husband just as Mr. Fellows stepped onto the servants' stair.

Mr. O'Brien lingered near a stand of trees on the long drive to the manor's front door. His expression, even from a distance, was one of hope and resignation all at the same time. I couldn't imagine what it must be like to wait years and years for news of a loved one. I could hardly wait to share what we had learned. Unladylike or not, I began to run, and Mr. O'Brien ran toward me.

I didn't give him a chance to bow or to waste time on a greeting. "Your Maggie did work here," I said quickly. "One of our maids remembered her quite well. And then one day she simply disappeared. We haven't discovered the cause, but we have found this!"

I reached out to hand him the box, only to have my arm stopped by an out-of-breath Mr. Fellows. He was glaring at poor Mr. O'Brien.

"What is the meaning of this?" he demanded. "If I discover that you are taking advantage of Lady Elizabeth and Lady Katherine in any way—

"You there," Mr. Fellows called to one of the gardeners, walking from the direction of the village. "Go and tell Essie Bridges to come here at once." Then he turned to my sister and me. "I have no doubt that she's put you up to this. I'm sure *you* have done nothing wrong."

"I can assure you, Mr. Fellows, that no one put us up to anything," I said, trying to match his dignified tone. "We only wanted to help a good, kind man find his wife."

Mr. O'Brien, Katherine, and I were all trying to explain, our words spilling over one another's in a jumbled mess. Mr. O'Brien could barely take his eyes off the box.

Essie ran up a moment later. Her shock upon seeing Mr. O'Brien led to disappointment when she saw the box and then looked at Katherine and me. She was about to say something to us when Mr. Fellows held his hand up, cutting her off.

"Pack your things," Mr. Fellows said. "You are to leave here before the day is over. You are dismissed from service. Without a reference."

Essie gasped. "Surely, Mr. Fellows, you can't dismiss me without a reference! I'll never find another position."

"No, Mr. Fellows," I cried. "You can't blame Essie."

"She didn't know," Katherine added desperately. "She didn't know."

Sean O'Brien, too, tried to plead Essie's case, but Mr. Fellows was unmoved, his face a mask of anger and indignation.

This was the scene that Papa came upon, alerted by the same gardener who had run for Essie. Papa silenced Katherine and me when we tried to explain what had happened. Mr. O'Brien was too cowed by Papa's presence to speak, and poor Essie was too distressed.

My stomach churned over all the upset I had caused while Mr. Fellows told his version of the story. I thought surely that Papa would be sensible and hear what I had to say, but he shushed me again. He was even angrier than our butler.

"To think that such a man has taken advantage of the generosity and kindness of two young ladies," he said, shaking his head. Then he turned to Essie. "And you helped."

Katherine began to weep while Essie tried to tell Papa that we had kept our deeds a secret from her.

Papa would not hear it. "Be grateful that your only punishment is losing your position," he said to Essie. "Fellows, send for the constable. I'll have this man arrested."

"No, Papa!" I said. "They have done nothing wrong—neither of them."

"My dear child, you must trust me in this matter. I know best."

Papa's dismissal made me angry. "No, Papa," I said. "You do not know best. Not in this matter."

I had never spoken to Papa like that before, and his shock rendered him speechless for a moment. I took advantage of his silence to say more—in a calmer tone this time. "Just yesterday you told Katherine and me that we are young women now, almost adults. Why can you not trust us to speak about this, to tell you what has truly occurred?"

"I have heard all I need to hear," Papa answered sternly.

I shook my head. "You have heard only what Mr. Fellows believes. That is not the whole truth."

Mr. Fellows huffed, but remained silent.

Papa waved his arm, as if to tell me to go ahead.

"I believed Mr. O'Brien," I said. "Everything about his story rang true. There were too many correct details for it to be the trick of a charlatan. We owed it to him to try to find out what happened to his wife."

"Essie didn't know," Katherine added, wiping her eyes. "When she was forbidden to pursue the matter, she told us we had to drop it, but we decided to go ahead without her—in secret."

"There is proof in your own staff ledger that Maggie O'Brien worked here and disappeared just when Mr. O'Brien stopped receiving letters," I said. "And the maid, Clarice, told us more."

Papa seemed to be actually considering what I had to say.

Katherine, emboldened by the change in his attitude, spoke up as well. "Mr. O'Brien is a good man, Papa. I know it."

I seized the moment, taking the box from Mr. Fellows and thrusting it into Mr. O'Brien's hands.

"This is Maggie O'Brien's box, and it belongs to her husband."

Essie, somewhat recovered, stepped forward. The sun caught on the Celtic knot that Katherine and I had given to her yesterday. "That's your mother's box, Lady Elizabeth. You told me so this morning."

"No, Essie. It's Maggie O'Brien's. I lied to you," I admitted. "We found it in the cellar, just where Clarice said it would be."

"I'm sorry it's locked, Mr. O'Brien," Katherine added. "We found no key."

Papa and Mr. Fellows finally saw that Katherine and I were correct about Mr. O'Brien. They tried to apologize, but the poor man was hardly listening. He cradled the box in his arms like a baby, but his eyes never left Essie and her necklace.

"There's the key," he said, indicating the Celtic knot.

"This?" Essie asked, touching the knot. "This is a charm! Lady Elizabeth and Lady Katherine gave this to me just yesterday."

"We found it in Mama's trinket box," Katherine explained. "We thought it would make a nice necklace."

Essie looked more closely at the small knot that hung from the ribbon. "Yes, I can see now that this is actually a key!" she said excitedly.

We had caught the attention of a couple of the gardeners and a curious groomsman.

"Come, everyone," Papa said, looking around. "Let's move into the library."

Once there, we were quiet as Essie took off her necklace and handed it to Mr. O'Brien.

I held my breath, watching him place the box on a table. He fitted the arrow dangling from the heart into the lock, and the box opened with a loud creak.

Inside were three letters. I could see Clarice's name in a clear hand on top of the first. Mr. O'Brien opened it and quickly scanned its contents, making quiet exclamations as he read. Finally, after what seemed like ages and ages, he shared its contents.

"It's dated the twenty-ninth of November, 1827. My Maggie discovered that she was about to have a child. She left word with this Clarice that she was going to the midwife in the village—a Mrs. Thornton. She wanted Clarice to send this letter to me if she did not return." Mr. O'Brien showed us the other letter, addressed to

Sean O'Brien in India in the same careful hand.

"She wanted her wages to go to the earl to care for the child until I could return."

Mr. O'Brien was overcome for a moment, and Papa led him to a chair. We all gathered around him. He opened his own letter and began to read. The letter seemed to fill him with joy and sadness, but he did not share its contents.

I was sensible to the man's distress, but I was also curious. "Who is the third letter to?" I asked finally.

"It's for her unborn babe," he said. He opened that letter too. "Essie was her favorite name," he said after a moment. "She wanted her babe to be named Essie if she was a girl."

I turned to our own Essie, whose face was pale. Surely she didn't still believe that she would be forced to leave Chatswood Manor. I led her to a seat.

"I don't understand. Why were these letters never delivered?" Papa asked.

"Maggie believed Clarice could read, because she tried to teach her," I answered as it dawned on me. "But Clarice only pretended to learn. She hid the box away to protect Maggie."

"I wonder what happened to her baby," Katherine whispered. "*Her* Essie."

Mr. O'Brien's eyes were locked on our Essie. I turned to her and saw that tears were streaming down her cheeks.

"Essie, what's wrong? What is it?"

12

"*I* was delivered by the midwife Mrs. Thornton on the evening of the twenty-ninth of November, 1827—the day these letters were written," she said. "The only things I know about my mother from the people who raised me is that she was Irish and that she wished for me to be named Essie." She raised her eyes tentatively to Sean O'Brien's.

"You're the spittin' image of your ma," Sean O'Brien said. "Of my Maggie. I thought so the first second I saw you, but I didn't dare hope."

Essie was speechless.

"You're Maggie O'Brien's daughter!" I said. "Oh, how wonderful!" I had been weeping a lot in these past few months, but today's tears were tears of joy. Essie had found her family. Her deepest wish was fulfilled.

"I hope you'll let me be your pa," Mr. O'Brien said.

"And get to know you like a father should."

Even Papa had to wipe away a tear as the truth of Essie's parentage was revealed. Mr. Fellows kept looking away and clearing his throat.

Katherine gave Essie a big hug. "You have the family you longed for, Essie. I'm so happy for you."

I joined in the hug too. "I'm happy too. Even if it means you have to leave us to go to Ireland."

Katherine and I both began sobbing harder now, the joy mixed with sadness over the idea of losing our beloved Essie.

"I couldn't love you girls more if you were my very own," Essie said, sobbing too. "But I long to get to know my father. Oh, I don't know what to do!"

"Fellows," Papa finally said, "surely we can find a position for Mr. O'Brien at Chatswood Manor. Families must be kept together. There's nothing more important."

Mr. Fellows nodded, blinking rapidly. "If Mr. O'Brien is willing, of course."

I held my breath until he answered. It was all I could do not to plead with the man.

"I'd be proud to," Mr. O'Brien answered.

Papa patted him on the shoulder. "We'll be proud to have you."

Mr. Fellows slipped out of the room, I imagine to get away from our excess of emotion. Katherine and I let go of Essie only to wrap our arms around Papa. "Thank you, Papa. Thank you," we said.

We watched Essie take a few shy steps toward her father and, with trembling fingers, take the letter that her mother had written to her.

"Take the rest of the day, please, Essie," I said, glancing at Papa, who nodded his consent. "Read your letter. Sit and talk in the garden."

"Thank you, milady," Essie said.

"You've done a wonderful thing in reuniting Essie with her father," Papa said, watching them leave. "Thank you for being brave enough to stand up for what you believe in."

"Oh, it was a grand adventure, Papa," I said. "Sneaking about, coming up with secret plots, finding hidden passageways. Except for having to hide things from you and Essie, I think I loved every minute."

Papa laughed. "I can't condone keeping secrets from your papa, but you do have an adventurous spirit." Then he turned to my twin. "What about you Katherine? Did you discover a love of adventure?"

"Oh, I think I've had quite enough secret escapades," Katherine said, laughing. "No more bold adventures for me."

I giggled. "At least not until you marry your pirate."

Papa drew us into his arms. "Something tells me, my dear daughters, that this is but the first of many secret escapades you will undertake together."

Every
Secrets of the Manor
book leads to another.

Read on for a first look at
Katherine's Story,
1848

I sat back in my deck chair, closed my eyes, and took a deep breath of sea air. No matter how many times I wished it, the paddle steamer *Britannia* would not stop rocking and rolling on the waves of the Atlantic. We could not reach America soon enough to suit my seasick stomach.

Opening my eyes again, I saw my twin sister, Elizabeth, at the deck rail, watching a school of dolphins. They had appeared suddenly after luncheon, leaping and dancing in the waves. They seemed to be performing for the entertainment of the ship's passengers, who surrounded my sister, laughing and calling out to the sea creatures.

I saw one leap above the white foam of the waves and squeal loudly enough for us all to hear. Was it saying hello?

Elizabeth made quick sketches in her drawing pad, catching the essence of the sleek creatures in a few simple lines. No doubt she would include the dolphins in her next painting.

She turned to me, still in my deck chair, my journal unopened in my lap. "Katherine, aren't they the most wonderful things you've ever seen?"

"They're splendid," I said, trying to focus on something other than the lurching in my stomach, but it was no use. The dolphins were indeed splendid, but I would have enjoyed them much more if I had been able to watch them from solid land. My bold sister felt no ill effects from the motion of the ship, but I had been feeling seasick almost from the first moment we stepped aboard the *Britannia*.

It was one of the few differences between us. Elizabeth and I were so nearly identical that when we were born only Mama had been able to tell us apart in an instant. The only obvious physical difference between us was in our hair: Elizabeth's was stick straight while mine fell in waves. That and the fact that Elizabeth was half an inch taller. My twin often joked that she would gladly give me her half inch in height in exchange for my wavy hair.

Right now I'd gladly give her my queasy stomach in exchange for just about anything of hers.

Elizabeth's face fell, seeing my discomfort. "Is it very bad today?" she asked.

I shook my head, not wanting to trouble her. "Not today," I said. "I'm grateful that yesterday's storm has passed, but I am rather tired. I believe I'll lie down for a while before dinner. I'll go and find Essie."

I stood and made my unsteady way toward the passage to our first-class cabin.

As if she had a sixth sense, Essie Bridges, our lady's maid, stepped onto the deck from belowstairs. Like the steadfast friend she was, Essie supported me as I walked shakily across the deck. Minutes later, I was safely ensconced in my bed in the stateroom I shared with Elizabeth.

Essie tucked me in and placed a cool cloth on my forehead. "It won't be long now, Lady Katherine," she said. "I expect you'll feel right as rain the minute your feet touch the dock."

"As long as it isn't moving," I said with a wry smile. "And to think I used to joke about marrying a sea captain."

"Marry a man with two solid feet on the ground, milady," Essie answered. "That's what my da always says."

I couldn't help but smile. Essie and her "da" had recently been united after a lifetime never knowing each other, and she had taken to quoting his wisdom at every opportunity.

Many years ago, Essie's mother, Maggie O'Brien, had been a kitchen maid at our family estate, Chatswood Manor. She kept the fact that she was married a secret from everyone at the manor. Her husband, Sean O'Brien, had sailed to India to earn his fortune. He'd planned to come home or to send for Maggie as soon as he could. Maggie had wanted to train to be a teacher—it was her deepest desire to teach children in her home country of Ireland how to read—and Sean O'Brien wanted to make her dream come true. But by the time he had enough money to send for Maggie, she had disappeared.

Sadly, we learned much later that Essie's mother had died in childbirth. She kept the fact that she was due to have a baby a secret even from her husband and slipped into the village one afternoon on her half day off to find the midwife. The midwife didn't even know the poor young mother's name, only that she was Irish and wished to name her daughter Essie. When the young woman died, a family in the village, named Bridges, agreed to raise the baby as their own, but they honored her mother's wish to call her Essie.

At Chatswood Manor, Maggie O'Brien was simply listed in the staff ledger as a maid who had worked in the kitchens for a few short months before disappearing one afternoon.

Essie herself entered service at Chatswood Manor when she was a teenager. Her warm smile and cheerful nature soon made her our favorite housemaid. When my sister and I were old enough to require a lady's maid, she was our first and only choice. Like Mama, Essie could almost always tell us apart, and she always knew just what to say when we were feeling sad or scared. She wasn't a blood relative, of course, but she was as much family to me and my sister as we were to each other.

When Maggie's husband, Sean O'Brien, came in search of his wife twenty years after she disappeared, Elizabeth couldn't resist the chance to solve a real-life mystery. My adventurous sister talked me into helping her find out what had happened to the mysterious kitchen maid. We had no idea it would lead to our dear Essie being united with her father.

It was a happy, happy day when we made our discovery. Essie, who had helped Elizabeth and me survive the death of our own dear mama, deserved all the happiness in the world. I wondered if she minded our pulling her away on a pleasure trip just a short while after she and her da had found each other.

"Do you miss your father very much, Essie?" I asked.

Essie nodded and gave her customary cheerful smile. "It's the first time we've been apart since we found each other," she said. "But this is a grand adventure, and I wouldn't want to miss a minute of it with my young ladies."

"Mama would have enjoyed it," I said quietly, placing a hand over my necklace.

Mama had died before Elizabeth's and my twelfth birthday, but not before she chose the most special birthday present I could ever imagine. On the morning of our birthday ball this past spring, Papa had presented me and Elizabeth with two velvet boxes. Inside, we each found a stunning gold pendant in the shape of half a heart. Mine was studded in brilliant blue sapphires, as blue is my favorite color. My sister's pendant was encrusted with red rubies, reflecting her favorite hue.

When the two halves of the heart are joined together, a secret compartment reveals itself. Elizabeth and I wrote a secret message to each other, cut the letters into confetti, and divided the pieces between the two necklaces. We promised to pass the necklaces along to the daughters we would have one day. We hoped that future generations of girls in our family would discover the secret message and be inspired to feel the same love for each other that Elizabeth and I felt for one another.